"Thought you were going to kiss her there for a minute," Mason said

Bandera watched the rearview mirror. Holly was getting on the back of her cousin's giant motorcycle. Even from this distance, it was easy to admire her nice long legs. "I never kiss women who practice seduction on the rebound," he said.

The motorcycle was coming up behind them, traveling at a good clip. It passed them, and Holly waved, her long hair flying out from underneath the helmet. Watching the motorcycle carefully, he passed, wondering why it was slowing. Holly waved at him, her eyes alight with mischief; she raised her fingers and shot something through his open window.

He snatched it from his lap.

Mason sat up to stare over the seat at the lacy white missile. "It's that thing the groom is supposed to throw to his groomsmen," Mason said, shocked. "Whoever catches it is next to get married." He recoiled as if the satin-and-lace circle might fly his way. "I've known grown men who wouldn't even be in the same room with a garter!"

Bandera met his brother's wide gaze in the mirror, his heart thundering harder than it ever had in his life. The satin felt slippery and unusual between his rough fingers.

"You *caught* it," Mason said. "I hope you're ready."

ABOUT THE AUTHOR

Tina Leonard loves to laugh, which is one of the many reasons she loves writing Harlequin American Romance books. In another lifetime Tina thought she would be single and an East Coast fashion buyer forever. The unexpected happened when Tina met Tim again after many years—she hadn't seen him since they'd attended school together from first through eighth grade. They married, and now Tina keeps a close eye on her school-age children's friends! Lisa and Dean keep their mother busy with soccer, gymnastics and horseback riding. They are proud of their mom's "kissy books" and eagerly help her any way they can. Tina hopes that readers will enjoy the love of family she writes about in her books. Recently a reviewer wrote, "Leonard has a wonderful sense of the ridiculous," which Tina loved so much she wants it for her epitaph. Right now, however, she's focusing on her wonderful life and writing a lot more romance! You can visit her at www.tinaleonard.com.

Books by Tina Leonard

HARLEQUIN AMERICAN ROMANCE

†Cowboys by the Dozen

BELONGING TO BANDERA
Tina Leonard

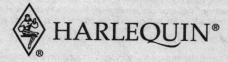

TORONTO • NEW YORK • LONDON
AMSTERDAM • PARIS • SYDNEY • HAMBURG
STOCKHOLM • ATHENS • TOKYO • MILAN • MADRID
PRAGUE • WARSAW • BUDAPEST • AUCKLAND

ISBN 0-373-75073-0

BELONGING TO BANDERA

Copyright © 2005 by Tina Leonard.

This edition published by arrangement with Harlequin Books S.A.

® and TM are trademarks of the publisher. Trademarks indicated with
® are registered in the United States Patent and Trademark Office, the
Canadian Trade Marks Office and in other countries.

www.eHarlequin.com

Printed in U.S.A.

THE JEFFERSON BROTHERS
OF MALFUNCTION JUNCTION

Mason (38), Maverick and Mercy's eldest son—
He can't run away from his own heartache or The
Family Problem.

Frisco Joe (37)—Fell hard for Annabelle Turnberry
and has sweet Emmie to show for it. They live in
Texas wine country.

Fannin (36)—Life can't get better than cozying up with
Kelly Stone and his darling twins in Ireland.

Laredo (35), twin to Tex—Loves Katy Goodnight, North
Carolina and being the only brother with a reputation
for winning his woman without staying on a bull.

Tex (35), twin to Laredo—Grower of roses and other
plants, Tex fell for Cissy Kisserton and decided her
water-bound way of life was best.

Calhoun (34)—Loves to paint nude women and he's
finally found Olivia Spinlove, the one woman who
holds his heart.

Ranger (33), twin to Archer—Fell for Hannah Hotchkiss
and will never leave the open road without her.

Archer (33), twin to Ranger—Sassy Aussie Clove Penmire
came all the way from Australia to Texas and took his
heart.

Crockett (31), twin to Navarro—He was the *first* artist
in the family! And he wants everyone to know it.

Navarro (31), twin to Crockett—Fell for Nina Cakes
when he was supposed to be watching her sister,
Valentine, who is the mother of Last's child.

Bandera (27)—Spouts poetry and has moved from
Whitman to Frost—anything to keep his mind off the
ranch's troubles.

Last (26)—The only brother who has become a new
father with no hope of marrying his child's mother.
Will he ever find the happy ending he always wanted?

Many, many heartfelt thanks to my friends, the Gal Pals and the Scandalous Ladies, for being an endless source of support and enthusiasm. Georgia Haynes, thank you for being such an awesome proofreader and cheerleader.

Much love to Lisa and DeanO, for being my best friends.

As always, thank you to the wonderful people at Harlequin and eHarlequin for giving me a career—especially Stacy Boyd, for keeping me focused and working!

Finally, many thanks to all the readers out there who have enjoyed the Jefferson bad boys— your support has meant so much to me!

Chapter One

Effort separates the quitters from the rest—
Maverick to his sons when they wanted to
quit studying the great classics and read
comics instead

"What I think," Bandera Jefferson said, "is that he
who lives by the sword, dies by the sword. Ernest
Hemingway, in a not too kind moment, if you ask
me."

"What are you blabbing about?" Mason, Bandera's oldest brother and head of the Jefferson family, demanded.

"I'm talking about our moved-to-town, much-
missed next-door neighbor, Mimi. If she, as the new
sheriff, wants you to be her deputy, you'd probably
be the happiest you've ever been, because the path
of the sword has always been your way."

Mason grunted. "That soliloquy was philosophical
and annoying all at once. And incorrect, I might add."

"I took the road less traveled," Bandera recited. "Frost, of course. I've been looking through Maverick's old books, and did you know Dad liked to underline famous quotations?"

"Which is why you have a healthy respect for them. That doesn't mean you know what you're talking about, though." Mason put his hat on before getting into his truck. "Famous quotations are only useful if you abide by their advice, Dad's notwithstanding."

"Where are you going?" Bandera demanded.

"None of thy business," Mason said, "quoting me, in my favorite conversational tone, Butt-Out-Ski."

"I don't like it. It's too lowbrow, not that I ever really understood the terminology of low and high brows. Where does a brow come into the picture, anyway?" Bandera murmured, his voice trailing off as he stared into Mason's truck. "Hey, you've got a duffel in there! Stuffed full."

Bandera remembered all too well the months that Mason had recently spent Lord knows where, leaving his younger brothers to run the family ranch, affectionately known as Malfunction Junction. "You can't go off and leave us again! We're bone thin at our place as it is. The ranch needs you. *We* need you." He frowned, staring at his brother, who clearly wasn't listening to him. "This is because of Mimi and that deputy stuff, isn't it? Mason, listen. If you don't want to run for deputy, tell her you're not interested. Tell

Mimi you'll help with her campaign and that's it. No more adventures. Say, 'Mimi, our high jinks are at an end. You and I are no longer wayward kids.' Quoth Bandera, from a trough of desperation, on an unseasonably hot Texas day in June."

Mason shook his head. "I need to talk to Hawk, and maybe Jellyfish."

"The phone's in the kitchen," Bandera said helpfully. "Or you can use my cell if yours is dead."

"Gotta be in person." Mason cranked the truck engine.

"A duffel means more than one or two days." Bandera blinked, thinking fast. What if Mason decided not to come back for months? His brother was under a lot of stress. It wasn't just the ranch—it was Mimi, too. Mason had never fully retrieved his heart from Mimi's clutches, and Mimi asking him to be her deputy wasn't sitting well. For Mason, it was temptation of the highest order, the thought of working daily with the woman he couldn't get off of his mind.

"Don't you leave this driveway," Bandera said. "I'm grabbing my stuff and going with you." Someone had to bring Mason back from the edge of madness.

"No." He began backing up the truck. Out of the window he said, "You need to stay here. There's work to be done."

But there was a brother to lose. There wasn't time to call a family council, and Bandera knew an emergency when he saw one. None of the other brothers would allow Mason to go off like this, not with him acting all secretive. A day or two of ranch-work minus two brothers was better than six months of Mason being off in the wilds, nursing his obtuse heart.

"If you move from here," Bandera said, standing up to his brother for maybe the first time in his life, "I will follow you in my truck. You will see me in your rearview mirror like a hound from hell on your tail."

Mason sighed, putting his vehicle in Park. "You're an idiot."

"Sticks and stones may break my bones, but words will never harm me," Bandera said.

"And if you recite one thing while we're gone," Mason said, "I promise to do you some type of harm."

Bandera loped off to get his stuff. In the hallway of the main house, he ran into his brother Crockett. "I just discovered Mason in the midst of another Houdini," Bandera said. "Not much time to talk, but go out there and stall him, okay? Just in case he decides not to buy my threats."

"What?" Crockett looked out the window.

"Just go keep him occupied!" Bandera ran up the stairs. He tossed jeans, boots, socks, a passport just in case—

His youngest brother, Last, came into the room. "Running away from home?"

"No, but I think Mason is. He's got his duffel in the truck and he's heading off to see Hawk." Bandera threw a toothbrush into his bag and dug around in his drawers for other things he might need.

"Why?" Last asked. "Can't he just call him?"

"Apparently not. Which is why I'm riding shotgun. Unless you want to go?"

"No, thanks." Last backed up. "I'll pack a cooler for you."

"Thanks." Running down the stairs and crossing the lawn, Bandera jumped into Mason's truck. "Crockett, you're a good man."

Crockett shrugged his shoulders as he leaned his forearms on Mason's window. "I'd go with you, but someone's got to work around here."

Mason grunted. "'Bout time you did something."

Crockett slapped his brother's hat down over his face. Mason moved it back into position.

Last slammed the truck bed after he put the cooler in. "Here's snacks. Stop and get more ice."

"Jeez." Mason looked at Bandera. "We're only going a few hours down the road. Do you think you'll need much more survival gear?"

Bandera pulled licorice strings from his pocket. "I'm good to go on the road less traveled. Frost, of course, again. I really like the wintry old poet."

"Damn it!" Mason gunned the truck, making Crockett jump back and Last hustle to the side of the driveway. "I swear I'll strangle you with your lico-rice. And then you'll die by your own sword."

"I can tell it's gonna be fun," Crockett called. "Goodbye, Huck Finn! See ya, Tom Sawyer!"

"Just a regular bunch of comedians," Mason mumbled as he pulled away from the ranch.

"So what's the adventure all about?"

"Maverick, our long-lost father," Mason said. "Why else would I need Hawk's detective talents and the help of his erstwhile loony sidekick, Jellyfish?"

"Jelly isn't loony," Bandera said. "He's existential, man."

Mason grunted.

"So what does Maverick have to do with anything? What do you think you can find now that you didn't before?"

"Nothing. But Hawk will be better at turning over rocks and running through dead-end signs than I was. I'm hiring him. Or them. Professionalism is what we need."

"Whatever." Bandera looked out the window as they passed the many miles of their ranch. "Mason, maybe we should just accept the fact that we're never going to know what happened to Dad."

He knew it was the wrong thing to say the second he said it, and Mason's silence was loud with disapproval. Only Mason could communicate censure so effectively without making a sound. Bandera sighed as he took in the picturesque view speeding past his window. "We have one pretty spread of land. I'm going to miss Malfunction Junction."

"We're only going to be gone a few days," Mason said. "It's not like you need your teddy bear or anything."

"I wouldn't make fun of sleeping with teddy bears," Bandera said. "If you were sleeping with *your* little Mimi-bear, you'd not be off trolling after the past."

"Lovely," Mason said. "Why don't you find your own bear and keep your nose out of my business?"

"Because I like your business," Bandera replied. "It's much more interesting than mine. All I know about my corner of the world is that I like it the way it is. Women only bring chaos, though I can sometimes appreciate a little lowbrow chaos."

"What are you talking about?"

"I like my women on the rowdy side," Bandera said. "Not too sweet, not too sour. Not too good and not too bad. Like a white frilly dress with a polka-dotted thong underneath—hey, look at that!"

Bandera craned his head to see the woman on the side of the road waving a large sign. She was wearing blue-jean shorts and a white halter top. If he didn't know better, he'd think the halter had polka dots on it, *big* ones. "Probably a car wash," he murmured. "Slow down, Mason."

"No," Mason said. "There's no time. This is going to be a fast trip. It's an information-seeking venture, not a woman hunt. Nor do I need a car wash."

They whizzed past so fast Bandera could barely read her sign. The blonde flashed it at him, holding it up high so that he got a dizzying look at her jiggling breasts. White teeth, laughing blue eyes and legs so cute he was sure the fanny she was packing had to be just as sweet. "Stop, Mason!"

His brother stomped on the brake, sighing. "Why couldn't you have stayed home?"

"That woman's sign says she needs assistance," Bandera said righteously, although he really thought it had read *I'm Holly.*

"And Lord only knows we never leave a lady without assistance." Mason glanced into the rearview mirror. "I sense trouble in a big way."

The lady bounced up to Mason's door. "Hi," she said.

"Howdy," Mason and Bandera said together. "Can we help you, miss?" Bandera asked.

"I'm waiting for my cousin," she said. "Obviously, you are not him."

Mason was silent. Bandera took off his hat. "Did your car break down, miss?"

"No." She smiled, and dimples as cute as baby lima beans appeared in her cheeks. Bandera felt his heart go *boom!*

"My cousin is coming to pick me up," she said. "That's why my sign says I'm Holly."

"I'm confused," Mason said to Bandera. "Nowhere on her bright white placard do I see the word *assistance*. Or even *help!*" He sent his brother a disgusted grimace.

"My cousin and I haven't seen each other in a while," Holly said. "He might not recognize me."

Bandera stared at her high-piled blond hair with fascination. It had pretty twinkly jewels among the strands, which matched the iridescent sequins scattered on the white halter top.

"Okay," Mason said. "You'll have to pardon us. We need to be getting along. Normally, we don't stop for ladies holding signs, but we thought you needed help."

"Actually, I do," she said. "I could use a kiss."

Bandera's jaw dropped. "A kiss?"

"Sure. I'd like just one kiss from a cowboy before I leave Texas." Her blue eyes laughed at him. Mason was far closer to her than he was, and that was a durn shame if she was wanting kissing.

"Why?" he asked.

"I'm feeling dangerous," she explained, "since I just left my wedding after I caught my fiancé in bed with my best friend."

"Ouch," Mason said.

"Precisely. So I called my cousin from the church

phone, and this is our meeting place. But now that you're here, I'm thinking a girl ought to be kissed on her wedding day," she said, looking at Bandera.

Bandera's heart gave a funny ding inside him. She sure did have kissing on the brain.

"So you're a bride on the run," Mason said. "Haven't we had one of those in our family?"

"That was a groom on the run," Bandera said dryly, giving him a pointed look. "Plural, actually."

"I'm not running, I'm going on a well-needed sabbatical," Holly corrected.

"Actually, you have an itch to get as far away from your fiancé as possible," Mason theorized.

"You understand me totally. I am trying really hard not to cry," Holly said. "You might have noticed my hair is done. My gown was chiffon and sequins— this is the top, the skirt I discarded—and I left the ring on the condom box I found on the kitchen counter."

"In the kitchen?" Mason asked.

Holly shrugged. "They'd moved to the bedroom and didn't hear me come into the house. There was a red bra lying in the fruit bowl and a trail of clothes leading into the den." She sighed and blinked her eyes quickly, which made her look like a doll. A doll trying not to cry.

"I think the condom box was the right place to leave your engagement ring," Bandera said, trying to be sympathetic. He really did not want her to cry. She was too pretty to be sad, he thought. *I would make her smile all the time.*

Mason groaned.

"So about that kiss…" Bandera began, unable to resist.

"Mike should have been here by now," Holly said. Her gaze sought the long, empty road behind the truck. A stray curl fell from her pretty upsweep and brushed along the back of her neck. Bandera watched her lips bow as she worried. What man would be stupid enough to cheat on a mouth that could pucker into a perfect plump bud?

"Guess we should be going, since she doesn't need a ride," Mason said uncomfortably.

"Not so fast." Bandera looked at Holly again. "Haste makes waste, you know."

"Who said that?" Mason demanded, his tone low.

"Some wise man." Bandera took a deep breath and turned to Holly. "Ride with us."

She peered into the truck to see him better. "With you?"

He shrugged. "Sure. Why not?"

"Why not indeed?" Mason said dryly. "We have nothing pressing."

"What about my cousin?" she asked.

At that moment a motorcycle pulled up behind Mason's truck. A loud gunning noise punctuated the arrival before the driver shut the engine off. A large, ponytailed man got off the bike and walked toward them.

"Cousin Mike?" Holly said.

"Yeah. Hey, Henshaw."

They embraced briefly before Mike looked at Bandera and Mason. "They bothering you?"

"No," Holly said hastily. "They thought I needed help."

He shook his head. "Your mother's going to be worried."

"My mother will understand," she said. "She wouldn't want me marrying a man with the morals of a…bull."

"Well, time for us to hit the road, Mason," Bandera said. He figured they should. She might be cute, but she had issues. "Too bad about the kiss, though."

"What kiss?" Cousin Mike demanded, bristling.

Though Bandera thought many men would probably want to kiss this beauty, he said, "No kiss here."

"I was feeling the desire to rebound," Little Miss Adventure said. "Love the one you're with and all that."

Bandera blinked, appreciating her recitation. She looked like a Holly. She looked like a rosebud. Gosh, he was certain she could be a Gertie May and he'd still find her ravishing. "You probably get kissed all the time."

"I've never been kissed by a *cowboy*," Holly said.

Mason's brows rose as he looked from his brother

to Holly. "Bandera, I'm going to let you drive. I need a nap."

"He's not the kissing type," Bandera explained.

"No, I'm not," Mason said, getting out of the driver's seat and into the back of the double cab.

When Bandera stepped out of the truck Holly's gaze roamed over his face. He smelled perfume and noticed she was dainty compared to him—a tiny bundle of femininity.

"I'd best go with Mike," she said, looking up at him with what he thought was awe. For the first time in his life, he realized he liked being tall. Sweeping her up into his arms would be no problem. Making love to her would be—

"My mother would be upset if I rode off with two strange men," Holly said.

His fantasy shot, Bandera eased behind the steering wheel and closed the door. He wanted to say that he thought he and Mason had less strangeness about them than Cousin Mike, but he figured that might not be suave. "We'll be off, then."

"Thanks for the offer, though. 'Bye, cowboy."

Bandera nodded, tipping his hat. "Best of luck to you." Putting the truck in Drive, he pulled away.

"Thought you were going to do it there for a minute," Mason said.

Bandera watched the rearview mirror. Holly was getting on the back of the giant motorcycle and putting a helmet on. Even from this distance, it was easy to admire her nice long legs.

"I never kiss women who practice seduction on the rebound," he said.

"Not when they have a Cousin Mike attached to them, anyway," Mason said. "That seemed like a high-risk scenario."

"Wonder why her fiancé was such a dope? Why do girls always hook up with losers?"

Mason grunted. "I think any comment at this point should be a sonnet from Wordsworth, but I can't think of one."

"Maybe Shakespearean tragedy." The motorcycle was coming up behind them, traveling at a good clip. It passed them, and Holly waved, one long blond curl flying out from underneath the helmet. "I hate tragedies."

"A runaway bride is a tragedy."

"A runaway anything is a tragedy. Trains, horses, *brothers*. All four-hanky events." Bandera stepped on the gas, and was soon gaining on the motorcycle once more. Watching it carefully, he passed, wondering why it was slowing. Holly waved at him, then raised her fingers and shot something through his open window.

He snatched it from his lap. All white. No black polka dots. His gaze flew back to the road, and to her, as she rode off up the highway once more.

Mason sat up to stare over the seat at the lacy white missile. "It's that thing the groom is supposed to throw to his groomsmen," he said, shocked. "Whoever catches it is next to get married, so the legend goes. I've known grown men who wouldn't be in the same room with a garter."

Bandera met his brother's wide gaze in the mirror, his heart thundering harder than it ever had in his life. The satin felt slippery and unusual between his rough fingers.

"You *caught* it," Mason said. "Hope you're ready."

Chapter Two

Bandera hastily dropped the garter into his shirt pocket. "I don't believe in superstitions."

"Maybe you should," Mason said. "What about the Jefferson family superstition? The Curse of the Broken Body Parts? If something hurts, you're in love? You could be in for some pain. Be forewarned."

Bandera grunted. "Nothing of yours hurts, and you're in love."

Mason sat back, silent. Bandera rolled his eyes. He couldn't concentrate on Mason and his problems with Mimi when the garter lay in his pocket. He didn't dare remove it and stare at it in front of Mason. That garter had been on Miss Holly's leg at one point, and he dearly wanted to take a closer look at any article of clothing that had adorned her. It was just curiosity, he told himself, but he wouldn't be a man if he didn't have a healthy dose of male interest revving his motor.

"Why do you think she threw it at me?" he wondered.

"Either she no longer wanted it, and thought you might like a souvenir of meeting her, or she was extending an invitation."

"To?"

"To follow her. Luckily, we don't fall for female wiles in our clan."

"Spoken too soon," Bandera murmured. "Looks like we have Harley trouble up ahead."

Mason stretched up to look. "I'm not one bit surprised. That garter is bad luck, and you'd be wise to hearken its warning unless you want a trip to the altar."

"That kind of trip I don't want," Bandera said, stopping the truck alongside the motorcycle. His heart beat with pleasure at the sight of Holly. He really hadn't figured he'd ever see her again. "And I don't believe in bad luck charms." Switching the engine off, he got out of the truck. "Need a hand?" he asked Cousin Mike, his eyes on Holly.

Mike bristled. "Not yours."

"Lovely," Bandera said. "We've met once and he likes me."

Holly shook her head. "He's generally personality-impaired. We love him anyway."

"Probably because you don't see each other often. But I'll try to remember his dysfunction." He stared at the motorcycle. "Nice machine."

"It's my baby," Mike said mournfully. "But moody, I'll admit."

Bandera shook his head. "Load it into the back of the truck. We'll give you a lift to the nearest town with a bike shop."

Mike scratched his neck. "I guess I'll have to take you up on that."

"Oh, good," Holly said. "This will be fun."

Bandera wondered. Mason wasn't inclined to be anything but superstitious, Mike was mourning his bike, Holly wanted to be kissed by a cowboy, and Bandera figured there had to be very little chance of that happening.

But he was going to keep a close eye on her. He did not like pain, especially where a woman was involved.

Holly went to the truck and slid in the back of the double cab next to Mason, before Bandera could help Mike get the Harley loaded. Mason looked petrified, and Bandera wondered if it would be too obvious if he asked his brother to drive so he could sit in back with Holly.

Yeah. Too obvious.

Sighing, he got in the truck. "Off we go," he said. "Fun, fun, fun."

HOLLY TRIED HARD not to watch as Bandera drove. Her gaze kept going to the rearview mirror, where she could see his eyes shaded by his hat. They were dark and mysterious, which she found appealing.

Her ex of a few hours had been blond and much thinner than Bandera Jefferson. Bandera was a very big, broad-shouldered man. Strength radiated from him, even from the sun lines around his eyes. She liked his squarish jaw and the way he looked at her like she was some curvy siren.

She could see her garter peeking out of the pocket of his denim western shirt. Why she had thrown it, she really couldn't say. Until today, impulsive gestures weren't her thing.

The garter had been stuck in her purse hastily as she'd grabbed things and left the church.

She'd only had time to scribble a short note for her mother and father, telling them that she was sorry and that she loved them. After guilt had hit her—she *was* leaving them to clean up the mess—she'd known in the next instant her mother would applaud her, her sister would be proud, and Daddy, well, Dad might just decide to put some sense into her ex.

She'd not written the *real* reason she was leaving. Her ex really wasn't up to Henshaw family wrath.

Some wedding planner I turned out to be, she thought.

But no, the wedding would have been beautiful. Everything had been just right.

It was groom-picking she obviously needed help with.

Silence descended over the truck as the four occupants wondered what to say to each other. Bandera's gaze met hers, and they both gazed quickly in opposite directions.

She glanced at Mason. His eyes were closed, but his jaw was tense. Then she looked at Bandera and found him watching her in the mirror again.

"Guess we interrupted your plans," she said.

"Somewhat. We didn't have a set schedule."

"I did." She looked at her French manicured nails. "But I'm changing course."

"Sounds like the best thing to do right now. How come you weren't at the wedding?" he asked Mike.

"I was headed there when I got the call that it was called off. Actually, I got about ten calls."

"How?" Holly asked, surprised. "I didn't tell anyone but you that I was leaving."

"Your mother called my mother, who called me. Then your mother called me. Then your father. Then your ex-fiancé called me."

"He did? They did? Why didn't you tell me all this?" She noticed Bandera was listening with rapt attention, though trying to appear that he wasn't.

"Because you surprised me when I picked you up and you were with these guys. I thought you might have gotten yourself into trouble."

"I never get myself into trouble," she said sternly. "And if I did, I'd know how to get myself out just fine. All I needed was a ride."

"Anyway," Mike said, "they called me after I was already on my way here to get you. Do you want to use my cell phone to call them?"

"I'll call Mom and Dad later." Chuck she was never going to call again.

"And Johnny?" Mike asked.

"His name was Chuck. What's to talk about?" she demanded. "I think some things don't require words."

"I agree," Bandera said, his tone way too cheerful. "Red bras in fruit bowls generally illuminate a situation better than linguistic artifice."

"Ah," Holly said.

"As does a ring left on top of a condom box."

Cousin Mike cleared his throat.

Holly looked at Bandera.

"I'm sorry," he said, as if only she could hear. "A lady like you deserves more considerate treatment."

Her heart seemed to curl up and die with mortification, yet she appreciated Bandera's efforts to comfort her. "It's all right," she said.

"No, it's not. Did you know that the cognitive area of the brain, the part that helps make appropriate decisions, is the last to develop? It may not happen in some brains until twenty-four to twenty-six years of age."

She blinked. "Are you making excuses for my ex? Are you saying his cognitive functioning was impaired?"

She thought she saw color rise up Bandera's neck.

"No," he said, "I'm saying you'll be older the next time you choose a man, and you'll know exactly what you want. This was obviously not the right man. And yes, he must have been cognitively impaired, not to mention character-stunted, to make a bad decision like that. I'm sure you couldn't see any of that, however. I bet he sold himself to you as a regular prince."

"He did," she said sadly. "But he was no prince at all."

"Precisely," Bandera agreed cheerfully. "Now, the difference between you and me is that you agreed to be married. I wouldn't dream of such a thing. My cognitive functioning will always be too impaired for me to select a wife."

"Peachy," Holly said. "And you're not too proud to admit it."

"No, I'm not. Did you know Confucius said that a gentleman has neither anxiety nor fear? I have both," he boasted. "When it comes to the idea of matrimony, I am both anxious and fearful. I admire that you were even willing to consider it."

"Do you study Confucius often?" Holly asked.

"I like quotes. They give me a point of reference in my life."

She looked at him thoughtfully. "Are you super-intelligent, or just full of hot air?"

"Hot air," Cousin Mike and Mason said in unison.

She leaned back and stared out the window. He probably *was* full of hot air. More than Chuck, even.

But Bandera did make her feel better, she admitted. It was the way he kept watching her—until she'd catch him, then he'd look away quickly—that told her he found her attractive. For a woman who'd found a bra thrown atop the bananas in her kitchen, it was some comfort that the cowboy seemed interested.

Of course, he probably sold every woman the wheelbarrow full of horse manure he was pushing. "Where are we going?"

"If I remember, there's a bike shop up in Sweetbriar, just thirty minutes from here. If not, Charley will know where we can take your Hog," he said to Mike.

"Thank you," Holly said. "For going out of your way."

"My pleasure," Bandera replied, his voice deep and sincere. Holly glanced back to the mirror, finding his gaze on her once again, and this time she didn't turn away. After a heartbeat passed, she quickly broke eye contact and went back to staring at the countryside, unable to acknowledge—or reply to—the masculine promise in his voice.

The very thought of his pleasure made her skin tingle. Made her glow inside.

She had to be crazy. She had to be suffering from canceled-wedding fever to even be looking at another man. She should be crying; she should be devastated.

Bandera handed her a tissue over the seat, which she took, but Holly knew she wasn't going to need it.

"How's your adventure so far?" he asked.

She met his gaze. "Getting better all the time."

A cell phone rang, and Mike answered it gruffly before handing it over the seat to her. "Want to talk to the groom? Last chance before we cross the county line."

She took the phone reluctantly, aware that Bandera was watching her every move, his eyes dark and hooded.

He wasn't even going to pretend not to be listening. Maybe he was more rat than gentleman, she decided. "Hi," she said, her tone not happy nor encouraging.

"Where are you?" Chuck demanded. "We're all in the church waiting on you!"

"Who is waiting?" She frowned, knowing that her side of the family all knew there was to be no wedding. Surely his family knew, too. How much room for misunderstanding was there in leaving your engagement ring behind?

"My whole family and all my friends!" Chuck said, his voice rising in anger. "My side of the church is full, your side is empty. There's not one single soul there, and I'm beginning to think that's very suspicious, considering we sent out two hundred and fifty invitations!"

She realized Mason could hear her ex's terrified voice when he pulled his hat down low over his eyes. There was only a foot of space between them, and he was obviously uncomfortable. "There's not going to be a wedding," she said, "at least not where I'm the bride and you're the groom."

"What in the hell are you talking about?" Chuck demanded. "Everyone is here! Waiting on you!"

"The minister?"

"Well, no. I'm sure he's around somewhere, though."

She breathed a sigh of relief. "Did you find the ring?"

"What ring?"

"The engagement ring you gave me. When you asked me to marry you and before you slept with my best friend."

Sudden silence met that comment. Glancing Bandera's way, she thought she saw a small grin hover around his lips.

"I did no such thing. I'm appalled you would even suggest it!" Chuck said, his tone self-righteous. "Is that why you're not here? You're standing me up in front of all my friends and family because of some stupid misunderstanding—"

"I was there," Holly said quietly. "There was no

misunderstanding. You'll find the ring on the condom box."

There was another silence. "Listen," he finally said, no longer trying to mask his annoyance. "If you had ever slept with me, if you hadn't been so intent on that no-sex-until-we're-married crap, I wouldn't have had to go someplace else to get what a man deserves!"

Everyone in the truck heard Chuck's shout. Mason promptly cringed and Mike gave a deep sigh.

She wondered how deeply embarrassment could sink into her soul. Then Bandera pulled to the side of the road, stopped the truck and reached over the seat to gently take the phone from her hand. She could still hear Chuck raging as Bandera held the phone up over the seat.

"Let me show you how to put the past behind you," he said kindly. "This is your past." He closed the phone with a snap and handed it to Mike, who put it in his pocket. "See how easy that was?" Bandera asked Holly.

She blinked. "Just like that?"

He shrugged. "Over and out."

She stared into his eyes, which were dark and warm and understanding. Something peaceful melted over her, soothing the dark, hurt places. "Thank you," she said.

"Again, my pleasure." He grinned. "Don't ever let

a man talk down to you like that. Now be a good girl and open that cooler your purse is resting on. Get Mike and Mason and yourself a beer, because you've all had a hard day."

"Are you talking down to me?"

"No." Bandera grinned. "I'm merely asking you to pass the boys a beer."

"I'll go for that," Mason said. "Whew!" He fanned himself with his hat.

She looked at him askance. "What?"

Mason frowned. "Your fellow was a bit of a whiner, wasn't he?"

A blush ran all over her as she remembered that everyone in the truck knew she hadn't slept with her ex-fiancé—he'd certainly shouted his complaint loud enough. She handed Mason a beer, and then Mike, who snapped the top off and took a long swig.

"I was thinking about getting married once," Mason said conversationally.

Holly thought she heard Bandera gasp. Her eyes met his in the mirror, but he quickly broke contact and stared straight ahead at the road. "Why didn't you?" she asked Mason.

He scratched his head. "I never did figure that out exactly."

"Oh?" Holly held the beer bottle between her hands, happy for the coldness to reduce the heat of her own mortification. She focused on Mason's story. "Wasn't the right time?"

"I suppose not."

She looked at Bandera. "What about you? You have a sad story, too?"

"Hell, no," he said. "My stories are all happy and they're going to stay that way."

"Really?" She leaned forward, her arms over the back of the seat, and looked at him thoughtfully. "Did you learn that from Confucius, too? The secret to eternal happiness?"

"No. I learned it from my family. Happiness was a survival skill."

She glanced at Mason, who sat unmoving, the beer bottle hovering near his lips as he took in Bandera's words. "That stinks," he said suddenly. "I never thought about it before, but you're right. Happiness *was* a survival skill, and I believe we all stunk at it."

"Oh, come on, we were happy," Bandera protested.

"We were something, but it wasn't happy."

"We were happy! Last was always telling us how good it used to be."

Mason merely shook his head and glanced out the other window. Holly caught Bandera's gaze on her and sent him a sympathetic look. Maybe their youth hadn't been as happy as they were pretending? "Thank you for picking us up," she told him.

"It was nothing. We had nowhere pressing to be."

"Although we'd like to get there eventually," Mason said with a growl. "You just reminded me why I travel light, without family."

Holly's brow puckered. "So we *are* getting you off track?"

"No," Mason said with a sigh. "Our tracks are never quite straight."

"That's right. Everybody out. Holly's going to sit up here by me, so that she can read the map for me."

"I'm not a very good map reader," she said quickly, "I'm afraid I'd get you even more behind than you are."

"Yes, but that's Mason time you're worried about," Bandera said. "My time is slow and easy."

She blinked, caught by his words and the drawl. Without consciously wanting to, she thought about sex. Slow and easy sex. Lots of it. With Bandera.

Whew. Not ten minutes after her ex had bawled her out for making him wait until the wedding.

Something was wrong with her. She definitely had rebound fever.

"I cannot read your map," she said decisively. *You represent the lure of the unattainable, and I am in a weakened state.*

Mike hopped out, taking his beer with him. "Out," he said to Holly. "Go read the man's map."

"Now, look," she protested. "I don't know that I

like traveling with three men who are developing caveman instincts!" Sitting next to Bandera was going to get her nothing but trouble. She had a funny feeling he had cracked her code: sensitive, brokenhearted female needs a little male attention, some savvy sweet talk, a little cowboy chivalry and, shazam! She's saved from a tragically unhappy ending!

"We're not cavemen," Mason said. "We're trying to treat you like the lady you are."

She hesitated. Mike shrugged. "I like them," he said to her. "Better than Chuck."

"We don't know them," she said. "And they're men."

"Ahh," the three men chorused.

"What?" Holly demanded.

"Man issues," Bandera said. "Even before the big breakup, you had man issues."

"You're a freak," she said, "and I'm going to read your map for you, just so you can have plenty of time to think over your own issues once I get us all good and lost."

"Drop me off at the bike shop before you lead us the wrong way," Cousin Mike said. "I fancy a card game with some fellow bikers."

She sighed and crawled into the front seat. "I have now entered the danger zone," she said, her tone a trifle mocking.

"You have no idea," Bandera declared with a grin.

Chapter Three

Holly stared at Bandera, her eyes huge in her face. He liked that—he could tell she was torn between laughing at his comment and thinking he was teasing.

Or wondering if maybe he wasn't teasing.

He could let her off the hook and tell her he was just trying to make her smile—better yet, laugh—but it was too satisfying to have her watching him.

There was something about her that he found highly intriguing. Was it her dumping her ex instead of causing a scene? Or maybe the fact that she'd made him wait, and when the fool hadn't she'd refused to compromise her standards?

Bandera had to admit he liked a strong woman. He liked a lady with sass.

More than anything, he liked thinking she hadn't loved her ex enough to fall for his game. Oh, he knew how men like that thought. A man's game went something like this: "if you won't, she will."

Only Holly hadn't.

To Bandera's thinking, for any man who couldn't conquer his woman, there was a better man who could—and that made her ripe for possession.

"Feeling better?" he asked Holly. He could see her fingers trembling as she stared at the map, and he knew she was nervous. Why?

Maybe he'd been teasing her too much. The Jefferson men were used to gnawing on each other's flanks, with jests, with bad moods, with whatever. Even Helga, their housekeeper, had learned to fight fire with fire when the Jeffersons got on her nerves. In the beginning, when she'd first come to work for them, the eleven younger brothers hadn't wanted her. Mason had. The other brothers had made her life pretty difficult, but she'd won them over in her wise way.

And sometimes she played a bit of dirty pool to make a point, which the Jeffersons had respected.

Mimi was a regular fire extinguisher of her own. The Jeffersons rarely messed with her; one, because she was generally leading the parade of mischief, pulling Mason in her wake; and two, Mimi knew very well the high-stakes art of revenge. Nobody got the best of her.

Bandera frowned.

"What?" Holly demanded, glancing up at him. Her eyes widened. "Why are you looking at me like that?"

"I'm not," he said gruffly, and refocused his gaze

on the road. Why had Mason confessed he'd once wanted to get married? Confessed to Holly, a stranger?

Bandera glanced again at the woman in question. She was biting her lip as she stared at the map, moving a finger up a road to chart its path. He really liked her full lips, and the way she was worrying her mouth was cute.

He'd like to take a bite of her.

He dragged his gaze back to the road once more, realizing instantly that this was no fight-fire-with-fire miss they had with them. Mason wouldn't have been stirred to confession if he hadn't sensed a fellow injured soul to confide in.

Holly might not have loved her ex like she should have—or she would have thrown a fit when Bandera had hung up on him; if anything, she'd looked relieved—but she was hurt by what had happened.

And that's when he knew: This was a woman who wouldn't look over her shoulder when a man hurt her. Hell, he ought to have figured that when she'd tossed her garter through the truck window. She was a great-escape type of girl. There was enough of that in the Jefferson family that he should have recognized the trait right off the bat.

And suddenly, he wanted to mend his ways. The urge to start over, to make her see he could do things right, was strong inside him. "Hey," he said, "I'm sorry."

"For what?"

"I shouldn't have said what I did. Maybe I shouldn't have hung up on your, uh, fiancé. It's possible I should butt out of your business."

"No," she said slowly. "I'm grateful. I didn't want to ever speak to him again."

"Say the word if you have second thoughts, and this truck can get you right back to your family."

"I'm good," she said. "I'm really feeling better now that I'm on the open road."

"It feels good to me, too," Mike said from the back seat. "There are cards in here."

"I feel like rummy," Mason said.

"Hot damn."

Bandera listened to the sound of shuffling behind him, wondering how he could say more without the peanut gallery witnessing it all. Before he could figure it out, Holly said, while studying the top of the map, "I want to go to Canada one day."

"Why?"

"I don't know. And Alaska. I dream of fishing in Alaska."

He couldn't say he had dreamed of that, exactly. "Maybe you'll get there some day."

"We were going to honeymoon in Cancun." She glanced up at him. "Do you know, I really didn't want to go to Cancun. I wanted to go somewhere and hike, but Chuck said that wasn't romantic. I guess it's not, is it?"

Bandera shrugged, thinking he could probably get romantic anywhere with Holly, if she was in the mood.

He frowned. Sex seemed to be ruling his brain, ever since the moment he'd met Holly. He had the strangest conviction that this escape artist shouldn't escape from *him*.

"Bike shop up ahead," he said. "I think you'll like this place, Mike."

"Just when I had a hot hand." Mike put the cards away. "Another time, Mason."

"Sure."

The four of them got out after Bandera parked the truck. Bandera helped Mike ease the Harley from the truck bed while Mason went to get the shop owner. Holly hung back, still staring at the map, so Bandera went over to join her.

"We're going to get there, don't worry," he said. "I wasn't serious about you having to read the map."

"Good. Because I'm not exactly sure where you're going. But it was nice of you to give us a ride here."

Yeah. So nice of him to think about sex the whole time he'd had her in Mason's truck. He looked at her pretty hair, the do she would have worn to be married, and the halter top, and the sparkly earrings, and something made him ask, "When will you come back this way?"

"I don't know." She folded the map, laying it on the seat. "Depends on where Mike's going. What about you? When will you be back in Texas?"

Bandera shrugged. "Couple days. I think. It's kind of hard to figure out Mason recently."

"He's so sad." She looked over her shoulder to where Mason and Mike were checking out the Harley with the shop owner.

"Sad?" Bandera touched her fingers, wanting one feel of her skin before he never saw her again. "How can you tell?"

"How can you not?" She looked at him funny. "It's like his soul is old."

"Yeah." Bandera nodded. "He's always been that way."

"Really?" She moved her fingers away from his ever so smoothly, but he still noticed her withdrawal. Ah, well, he knew he'd been pushing his luck. He just hadn't been able to help himself. She was so unlike any woman he'd ever met. "I hope I didn't offend you in any way," he said. "I don't always know how to treat a lady."

"I thought you did fine," she said softly. "You took my mind off the whole wretched matter, and somehow, I feel much better." She looked at him. "I thought I was going to die of mortification, and now that I've met you, I'm pretty sure the best thing that could have happened did."

He grinned. "I'm sure you're right."

"Can I ask you a question?"

"Shoot." *Let it be the magic question,* he thought. *Yes, you can have a ride in my truck, anywhere you want to go.*

She took a deep breath. "Would you marry a girl who didn't sleep with you before the wedding?"

He was dumbstruck. Was she proposing? No, she wasn't. He shook his head to clear it.

"I didn't think so," she said. "Maybe I sabotaged my own wedding—"

"Wait," he said hastily. "I haven't answered yet. I was thinking."

"You were shaking your head."

"Yeah, but I always shake my head when I think," he said. "I haven't ever been asked that question. It requires thought, maybe even Confucius-style pondering. Deep thought on a mountain in China for years."

"No, it doesn't," she said. "It's either yes or no."

He stared at her, his mouth drying out. *No,* his mind said, *I could not wait until a wedding to have you, if you'd been my girl. I would have had you before the wedding, after the wedding and maybe during the wedding. I definitely would never have let you out of my sight.*

But yes, his more intelligent side argued. *If that's what it took, I would wait.*

He gulped. "This is one of those Gordian knot, only-the-Sphinx-knows kinds of questions. It has moral implications, and superhuman qualities involved." Was that sweat he felt on his brow, warming under his hat? He sensed that his answer meant a lot to her; she was trying to figure out how much a man would sacrifice for love. She wanted to know if any man loved deeply enough to wait.

He thought he felt a seam split in his jeans underneath his zipper. "Truthfully," he said, his voice tight, "I don't think I can answer your question. I'm sorry."

She nodded. "It's all right."

He'd failed. He had not sounded wise, intriguing or even honest. The answer was no. He could not wait. He wouldn't sleep around on his woman, but he certainly would not sleep without her, either. And that was just the way it was. When he met the woman for him, he was going to satisfy her so much she never thought twice about whether loving him was the right thing to do.

Holly's gaze wandered over his face. There was something between them, a flash of interest neither of them was sure about.

"Listen," he said, "I'm going to be real honest with you."

"Shoot, cowboy."

"All right. I wouldn't wait. Not one day, not one hour, not one second."

Her eyes widened. Then she blinked with surprise.

"And neither would you if you were really in love." He took a deep breath. "How do I know you weren't really in love? Because you hit the back door the first opportunity you could. You didn't even give him a chance to explain, not that he had a good answer. You just took to the road. Which tells me you weren't ready for this." He touched one light curl from the fancy wedding do. "That's cool, but you ought to be honest with yourself so you don't fall for the wrong guy again and have to use sex as a safeguard to keep your emotions where you want them."

She looked down. "I'm a wedding planner," she said. "Is it possible I just wanted a wedding of my own? The perfect dream? That's what's worrying me." Her gaze rose to his. "I hate that thought. It's so shallow. But I'm old enough to want some stability. A man of my own. Children. You know, I've lived other people's dreams. Now I want to live mine."

"Hey." He held up his hands. "I'm right there with you. There's been enough weddings in my family recently to last a lifetime. Wedding marches, flying rice and multiple 'I do's' have left me feeling like I'm the last man standing in a sea of change. The best poetry in the world can't stave off the feeling that I'm turning into the old man and the sea, with the tide turning against me. How weird is that?"

"So you feel left out?" she asked.

"Left behind. Don't tell Mason, but he does, too. Man, he's got this itch for our former next-door neighbor, Mimi, he ain't ever gonna scratch. When we Jeffersons mess up, we mess up big time."

"Why doesn't he just fix it?"

Bandera chewed on the inside of his cheek, noting that her fingernails had a pretty polish on them, like half-moons of white. Her wrists were small and dainty. She had the hands of a woman who spun dreams for other people, he decided. "Some things are not meant to be fixed. And then sometimes they're meant for another time. But you're not the only one who uses the open road to navigate through your emotions."

"Thanks." She smiled at him. "For putting that so kindly."

"Yeah. So. Looks like the Harley's working."

She turned around. "Hey, it is." Sliding down from the truck seat, she accidentally slid right into arms he put up to catch her. They looked at each other for a moment, Bandera recording the feel of her as fast as he could. The smell of her, the temperature of her skin, the silk of it, her height and how very, very good she felt.

"Whoa, I'm sorry," she said, stepping away. "I didn't mean to—"

"I did," he said, "and I'm not apologizing. And

I'm not saying sorry for this, either." He kissed her, his lips touching hers ever so gently, ever so briefly.

But long enough for him to know that this woman was supersweet.

He looked at her, reading shock in her expression. "Just as good as I thought," he said.

She didn't move. For an instant, he wondered if she was going to slap him. Tell him off. Call Mike to save her from his clutches.

But then she surprised him. Grabbing his shirt collar, she pulled his face back down to her level. She put her small, cool hands on both sides of his face, and she kissed him, using her body and her tongue and her lips to blow his mind.

When she released him, it was his turn to stare at her.

"*Now* I've kissed a cowboy," she said.

And then she walked away.

He watched her, his eyes hooded, as she went to her cousin. Mason appeared beside Bandera. "Pony up," he said. "The bike's back in business, and we have done our Good Samaritan duty."

Bandera stood silently, staring at the woman who'd just kissed him like he'd never been kissed before.

"Why have you got that dumbstruck expression on your face?" Mason demanded. "Indigestion? Solve the world's greatest mystery?"

"No," Bandera said. "That bride on the run is a woman just begging to be slowed down."

"Nah," Mason said. "She's not your type. No polka dots."

Bandera shook his head, his brain fairly ringing from all the signals he was receiving from Holly's kiss. "She is a reversible pattern, I do believe. It's just not obvious to the insensitive eye."

"Oh, jeez." Mason sighed, getting into the truck. "Can we stay on task here? We did have a mission, and it had nothing to do with your love life."

"I don't have a love life." *But maybe I should.*

Probably not. If there was one thing he'd learned from watching his brothers fall, it was that a woman was the road to matrimony. Holly was a wedding planner. That was a no-brainer danger signal, right? How close could a man dance around a fire without getting burned?

It was best to stay away from flammable things, for certain, and Holly was too hot for a man whose heart was used to staying pretty cool. She was geared to have weddings on the brain, either hers or someone else's. He patted his shirt pocket, which still contained the garter.

Walking around to the driver's seat, he said, "All right. You be map reader."

"Now you're talking." Mason relaxed, putting his seat belt on. "For a minute there, I thought you were doomed."

"Bandera!" Holly called.

Mason's eyes met his as Bandera hesitated in the midst of getting in the truck. "Act like you didn't hear her, just to be on the safe side," Mason said. "Maybe it's best to get in, lock the door and drive away."

"The shop's got an extra bike," Holly said, coming to stand next to him. "Mike wants to know if you want to rent a motorcycle and caravan to wherever you're going. The owner's in the mood to see the countryside with some buddies, and you're the only easy riders who've been by today who know their Hogs."

"A Hog for rent?" Mason perked up. "Really?"

"Mason," Bandera said. "Stay on task."

"Let me see this Hog he's renting." Mason got out of the truck, striding over to where Cousin Mike stood.

Bandera glared at Holly. "Mason has no business biking."

"Are you afraid of motorcycles?" she asked. "Mike seemed to think you and Mason might enjoy traveling that way as a novelty."

"I have plenty of novelty in my life, thank you," he said. "You've now got my brother off his path, and the problem with that is that I only came along to keep him on track." Holly just didn't understand the dilemma. "See, Mason has a tendency to wander. He wanders off, and when he does, he may wander off for months."

"Does he have an attention deficit disorder?"

"No, it's just…" Bandera sighed. "Look. I'd feel better if I could keep Mason in my sights at all times. With any luck, I'll have him home in two days, which will be a Mason record."

The sound of motorcycles gunning made Bandera swivel around. Mason was on the back of the biggest, flashiest Hog Bandera had ever seen. Mike was slipping on a helmet, and the shop owner—who Bandera realized with some horror was a tall, thin, rangy-looking brunette with foxy eyes—loaded herself onto the back of Mason's seat.

"Oh, no," Bandera said. "This is not going to happen. This is bad. No. Wait!" he yelled over the engine noises. "Mason! Hell, no!" He went running toward them, but Mike, Mason and the brunette waved and roared off. "Damn it!" Bandera tossed his hat to the ground. "Damn it to hell!" The glare he sent Holly should have shriveled her, but she drew herself up to her full height and turned her back on him, arms crossed.

Uh-oh. Now she was mad, and being alone in the countryside with a hot, angry female was not a recipe for happiness. He took a few deep breaths. "This is your fault," he said. "I'm sorry I lost my temper, but you shouldn't have dangled bait like that in front of Mason's face."

"If you'd been paying more attention to the discussions and less to your map fear, you would have met the shop owner and seen how nice she was," Holly said, annoyed. "Mike knows her. Apparently, she bought the business recently from the guy you knew."

"I meant the bike," he said crossly. "Mason and anything that gets him on an open road these days is dangerous. And that Hog was about the most alluring bait he's seen in months."

"Well, then he probably deserves it," she said huffily. "Maybe he doesn't like you being his ball and chain. I know I wouldn't."

Bandera stared at her. "Ball and chain?"

She turned around. "Frankly, your possessive attitude grates on my nerves."

He blinked. "Possessive?"

"Yes. You should be happy for your brother."

The brunette had been quite a looker. Very Cher-like, in her younger days. And she'd let Mason drive her Hog. He sighed. "Mimi isn't going to like you," he told Holly. "I'd watch that rhetoric around her."

"Who's Mimi?"

"The next-door neighbor. Well, used to be."

"Well, she's not here. And you gotta live life to the fullest, as I've learned only too well today."

"I know that quote," he said. "But I think there are varying definitions of what living life to the fullest means."

"Mike has a cell phone," she reminded him, "and

we can follow them to wherever you were planning to go in the first place."

"True." Bandera began to feel better. "Yes. Nothing to worry about."

Somewhere a door slammed loudly, making them both wheel around. He grabbed Holly and held her against him.

"Are you always nervous like this?" she whispered.

"Shh!" He'd thought the shop owner was the only person working in the place. She'd hung up a Closed sign in the window. He and Holly had seemed to be alone on miles of deserted country road. "I'm going to go make certain everything was locked up."

"Okay." She began walking and he pulled her back.

"No," he said, "I'm going to check, and you're going to stay here."

"Bandera! I just canceled a wedding! I think I can check to make certain a door was closed properly."

"I can't allow you to get in trouble out here."

She sighed. "Come on, cowboy. I never dreamed you'd be so needy, or I wouldn't have kissed you."

"More on that later," he said. "Stay behind me."

"What*ever.*"

He walked to the door, which had an old screen covering. It looked as if the brunette lived in the front part of the house and ran her business from the garage. He took hold of the handle, giving it a good shake, and the door swung open.

He and Holly exchanged glances.

"Not a good sign," he whispered. "I really did think this door slammed."

"I did, too. Go on in."

"No!" Bandera said. "It's her house!"

"And she'd appreciate you making certain nobody walked inside!"

Holly had a point. "Will you stay out here?" he asked.

Her eyes got big. "What do you think?"

"I think hell no."

She pushed him inside. Then she followed, glancing around. "Oh, it's so pretty," she murmured. "I love yellow-and-green gingham."

It looked like rays of sunshine had been splashed throughout the den. Plants were everywhere, blooming lush and green. The sofa was overstuffed and the chairs were fat leather recliners. "She didn't seem like the kind of girl who decorated comfortably."

"She seemed fine. I don't know why she's bugging you so much."

"Because she drove off hanging on to my brother's backside. I'm telling you, that wasn't in the plan."

"Today is not the day for plans. I'm going to call my mother," Holly said, crossing into the kitchen. "Look! She baked chocolate chip cookies."

"You yak, I'll eat." He perched on a flower-painted bar stool and made himself at home with the yellow-gingham plate. "Mmm. Maybe better than wedding cake. You should have one."

Holly rolled her eyes, but took one from him, being very careful to avoid his fingers, he noticed. Dialing the phone, she stood on the opposite side of the bar, instructing the operator to make a collect call.

He went to the cupboard and got himself a red coffee mug, which he proceeded to fill with milk, listening to Holly with only half an ear. A gray cat wound itself around his boot, startling him. "I think I found the door slammer."

"Cats don't slam," she said.

"This one does, when it wants past the screen. You little devil. I don't think you're supposed to be in the house, are you?"

It jumped onto the counter, looking at Bandera's cookies with interest. "No sweets for you," he said, putting her on the floor. But he poured milk from his coffee mug into her saucer to take the sting out of his comment.

"Softie," Holly said.

"An illusion," Bandera said. The cat settled down to lapping milk contentedly, and Bandera got back on his flower-covered perch, watching Holly as he helped himself to cookies.

She had a really fine figure. He wasn't certain he'd fully observed how nicely her waist curved into her butt, but now that she was leaning against the

counter, he could get the whole picture. He ate another cookie, happily enjoying the view.

"Hi, Mom," Holly said. "Yes, I'm fine. I really am.
I just wanted to apologize for leaving you to clean
up the mess."

She listened for a few minutes. "I'm glad, too, actually. It wasn't the right time. It's a shame everything went to waste, though. All the beautiful flowers
you— What?"

Bandera perked up, hearing the note of surprise in
Holly's voice.

"Oh. Well, I'm glad everything worked out then.
Okay. I'll call you from the next stop. I think I'll keep
traveling for now. Thank you. I love you, too, Mom.
Give Dad a hug and kiss for me."

She hung up and turned around, her eyes round.
"Chuck got married."

Bandera blinked. "The ex?"

"Yes." She started to giggle. "I know I shouldn't
laugh, but it's funny. He married my best friend. He
said all his friends and family were already at the
church, and the flowers, and the minister, and the
food had been catered, and it was all done wonder-
fully, and he wasn't going to waste it. He paid my
folks for the expenses and got married."

"What about the license?"

"Well, they're taking care of that now, Mom said,
by going on our honeymoon trip to Cancun. They can

get officially married there. I'm sure Chuck worked out all the details. He's good at that."

Bandera stared at Holly. "Are you upset?"

She shook her head. "Strangely, I'm relieved."

"I guess your best friend must have liked what you planned." He scratched his head. "Most brides like to pick everything themselves."

"I think she just wanted to get married." Holly shrugged.

"Are you sure you're all right?"

She nodded. "I was all right when you told me I hadn't really loved him."

He grunted. "Glad I could help."

"If you're through snacking, maybe we should go." She glanced around the room. "The biker lady really does a nice job of decorating."

"Yeah." He didn't care too much about that. Right now, there were other things to think about. "I can take you back home, if you want, since the coast is clear."

She smiled. "Thanks. But I think I'll ride with you as far as you're going."

"And then what?"

"Then I'm going to keep on going. For a while, anyway." She headed out the door. He pushed the bar stool up to the counter and hurried after her.

"Do you think the cat will be all right?" he asked, closing the door tightly behind them.

"I think her owner wouldn't have left her if she didn't have provisions made for her."

The little cat *was* in very good condition. "That's true. So, how long are you going to keep on going?"

"Well," Holly said, getting into the truck, "I spent nine months planning the wedding of my dreams, and working, too. I'm going to take a vacation and see the countryside. Then I'll decide."

Starting the engine, he drove away from the little bike shop. "I've got to get Mason home as soon as possible, or I'd join you."

"Oh, no," she said, "I'm doing this myself. I just got rid of one man. I don't want another."

"Well, it's not like I would interrupt your flow or anything," he said. "I'm in the mood for a little traveling myself."

She opened her purse and pulled out a lipstick. She applied it as she looked in the mirror.

He'd never seen a woman put on lipstick in a truck. It was very sexy, he realized uncomfortably.

"You have to understand," she said, "I'm never planning another wedding. Ever."

He tried to watch the road, but when she spritzed a light fragrant scent down her halter, his fingers tensed on the wheel. "I wasn't asking you to marry me," he said, "especially since you don't share my belief in premarital sex."

She laughed. "Believe all you want."

"How do you know you'll never plan another wedding? Yours or someone else's?"

"I'm going into a new business. And the next time I get married I'm not planning my wedding, I'm just going to do it." She snapped her fingers. "Just like *that!* He asks, I say yes and we go to…a justice of the peace or something. I think I'm good at planning," she said, "and maybe not executing."

"Ah. That makes sense." Bandera had experience watching his brothers with that same kind of problem. Although some of them had become pretty good at executing. "What business will you do now?"

"I haven't decided, but," she said, putting her purse away and pulling out the map again, "if that woman can run a motorcycle shop, I can do something beside plan weddings. I'm changing my whole life."

"Hmm."

She glanced up at him. "And you?"

"My life is fine. But I really didn't have an epiphany like you did. I just enjoyed the cat and the cookies."

"Yes, you did. Which surprised me. I didn't see you being such a hearth and home kind of man. I thought cowboys were adventurers of the West."

He sighed. "I do not want to adventure. I want to find my brother and get him home. He's the adventurer in the family, and it's really getting me down. If he'd just stay in one place—"

"Oh, broken hearts sometimes mean traveling feet. I'm a prime example." She tapped the map. "All these squiggly lines on here represent destinations I've never been. So I'm going."

"But your heart's not broken," he said, hoping he was right. He really didn't want her thinking about ol' Chuck. The only reason Bandera could think about her ex with any degree of rationality was because he knew the poor sap hadn't traveled to any of her physical destinations.

Like that fanny he'd been examining earlier. It was virgin territory, so to speak—unclaimed, unconquered.

He really, really liked thinking about her that way.

"But it could have been broken," she said, interrupting his spell. "I just got lucky that you came along."

"Lucky?"

"Well, you're so much more fun than Cousin Mike. I'd much rather travel with you." She smiled at him, and dimples blossomed again beside her lips.

Bandera's heart jumped. Dimples and a sexy butt.

Except she had him in the same traveling-companion category as Cousin Mike. That wasn't good for his ego.

"Look," he said, "your cousin was okay, but I'm not your cousin. Or your friend. We're strangers."

"True." She began pulling the twinkly things and pins out of her hair. Strand by strand, her hair came down. He gulped nervously. He'd never watched a woman take her hair down before. It was an awful lot like a prelude to taking off her clothes.

He really wanted her to consider taking off her clothes for him.

"But I feel safe with you," she said. "Somehow you seem almost like family."

"You're wrong," he said. "Think of me more as the big bad wolf waylaying you on the way to Grandma's house."

She reached to release another strand. "But you rescued me. I can't envision you as the big bad anything."

Yeah, well, his mouth was dry from thinking about all the tempting charms she had under her top and shorts. She had sexy legs and—

"You don't look like you feel well," she said, putting her hair doodads in her purse. "Your eyes are glassy."

He glanced away. "I'm all right."

"Do you want me to drive so you can rest?"

"I'm fine!" he snapped. "At least I was until you got my mind off my responsibilities."

"Look at that!" she exclaimed, pointing up ahead. "Hot air balloons!"

Two brightly colored hot air balloons floated over the highway. Bandera squinted up at them. "There must be a festival somewhere, because there's another one over there."

"I want to ride in a hot air balloon," she said softly. "I want to float for a while and gaze down on the beautiful earth."

He looked at her. He reminded himself of the task at hand, bringing Mason home. And he drove past the grounds where a steady stream of vehicles were turning in to the Berryland Hot Air Balloon Festival.

Holly didn't say a word. She just stared out the window at the balloons, the dogs on leashes and the casually dressed people enjoying a day at the fair.

Bandera gripped the steering wheel. He estimated he was about an hour behind Mason. If he kept going, he could probably get to Hawk's right after Mason did.

Holly reached back into her purse, pulled out a ponytail holder and put her hair up. Bandera's throat dried out again as he looked at the curve of her underarm and the softness of her skin as it peeked from under her tank top.

Just a hint of breast showed delicately from the armhole.

He sighed and turned around. "You're getting me way off my schedule."

She smiled as they entered the grounds. People lingered, pushing strollers or eating hot dogs. He parked the truck, trying not to think about the fact that Mason was getting far ahead of him, or the fact that his brother had no reason to turn around and head home when he had a sexy brunette clinging to him.

"Look," Holly said, clutching Bandera's arm. "That balloon is for hire."

"Yeah." He nodded without enthusiasm. "Anybody who'd go up in that thing is mad. Crazy. Completely off their rocker."

She let go of his arm and walked in the direction of the balloon, throwing a teasing glance over her shoulder. "I'm crazy."

"I know," he said, striding to keep up with her, "but not that crazy."

"I think you're crazy, too. Any man who breaks into someone's house and eats their chocolate chip cookies has a crazy streak."

"I was protecting her dwelling," he protested, trying to grab Holly's hand. "It was the least I could do since she's taking care of my brother."

Holly avoided him and ran to the balloon. He stopped mulishly in his tracks. If she wanted to do something risky, that was up to her. He was not her keeper. He was not her anything.

He watched her pay. He watched her put a leg over the edge of the basket as a man with a long ponytail helped her in. Bandera watched her look toward the sky with anticipation…and he realized he couldn't stay rooted to the ground forever. "Wait!"

Grabbing his wallet from his pocket, he ran to the balloon. "I'm with her," he said breathlessly.

"I know," the ponytailed man said with a grin. "She already paid for you."

"You minx," Bandera said to Holly, surprised.

She laughed.

The balloon's owner grinned. "She said you wouldn't be able to resist a challenge."

He wasn't. He climbed into the basket. "This is not what I thought I'd be doing today."

She smiled. "Me, either."

That was true. "I suppose you deserve a balloon ride after what you've been through."

"Everything about me is rising now," she told Bandera. "My spirits, my happiness—"

"And this balloon." He glanced worriedly over the edge. "We're actually going *up*."

"Yes," she said. "Did you think we would remain on the ground?"

"I don't know." They floated past the balloon owner's head, then ten feet higher. "Are we tethered to something? Because I'm not sure how to work one of these amusement rides."

"The owner is covered for disaster." Holly laughed at him. "You won't get hurt, I promise."

"I better not get hurt," Bandera said. "We have a healthy superstition about that in my family."

"Oh? You don't strike me as the superstitious type."

How little she knew. "Just being around you is attracting all kinds of karma into my atmosphere," he said. "My inner tuning fork is vibrating with danger."

"You do have a problem." She glanced over the edge, smiling. "Look! Everyone down there looks so small!"

"I'm not looking," he stated. "When do we get reeled back in? This has been fun, but not so much I couldn't stand to get my boots back on earth."

"Well," Holly said, her voice sounding a bit worried, "I think you'll have to settle for your boots lifting heavenward for a while." She pulled a rope in over the edge, settling it in the bottom of the basket, then she stood at the rail, waving. "By the looks of their faces down there, this rope was not supposed to come loose."

Small trails of dread slithered through Bandera's stomach. "I can't look. I just discovered I have a fear of heights."

She looked at him, concerned. "You do?"

"I think so. I've never been higher than the back of a bull. I've never even been to Six Flags to ride the roller coasters. I don't mind the second floor of the barn, but I suppose that's different."

"Very different. Barns don't float away, except maybe in *The Wizard Of Oz.*"

"Oh, jeez." He closed his eyes, trying not to think about the tiny blowing flame above his head keeping the balloon aloft. Hard ground lay below, and

Holly was at his side, staring up at him as she clutched his arm.

"You're not going to faint, are you?" she asked, her voice sweet and worried. "I really wouldn't advise it in this basket."

He noted her hands felt good on his arm, and the concern in her voice made him feel better. Still, he was in trouble. "I feel very out of control of this situation."

"Well, you are out of control, which is okay if you relax," she coaxed. "Keep your eyes closed if it helps."

Because she told him to keep his eyes closed, he snapped them open to stare down at her. Looking at her made him feel a whole lot better. "When we crash-land in some trees—and I'm sure that's the only possible ending to this dilemma I find myself in—you're going to be in big trouble. As soon as I get out of the hospital."

She laughed at him. "We're in this together. Enjoy the adventure until we crash."

Chapter Four

Holly knew she should take pity on Bandera—he really did appear terrified—but she sort of liked the way he was leaning on her instead of being withdrawn and cocky. "Remember when I got into your truck and said I'd entered the danger zone?"

"And I said you had no idea?"

"Mmm. Looks like we reversed roles."

He sighed. "Actually, no. You disturbed everything in my aura when I saw you by the side of the road, flashing your sign."

"I wonder if our meeting was something more than chance."

The look on his face was priceless, but Holly held back a laugh. If she was going to enjoy baiting him, she wanted to do it to the fullest.

"Meaning what?" he demanded.

"Think about it. You're in a balloon, far from safety, with a wedding planner."

He frowned. "Yes. That makes you a bride in flight."

"I'm not really," she said. "You rescued me from all that."

He stared at her. "All that what?"

"The trauma. The broken heart. The barren field of dreams."

"Yikes. I was trying to keep Mason from leaving us. I wasn't looking for a dramatic woman in white."

She laughed. "Admit you're having fun."

"No."

"And you liked it when I kissed you."

He slid his eyes back her way. "Lady, you are alone with me in a basket, apparently on your way to some unknown destination. Do not tempt what you know nothing about."

"Maybe I like the unknown."

His gaze warmed. "You'd best figure out how to keep yourself safe," he growled. "The possibility of crash-landing is not your only worry."

"And if I'm tired of being safe? If minding the rules didn't get me anywhere and I feel like throwing caution to the wind?"

"You might find your caution caught," he said.

Her heart pounded, and suddenly, the scenery outside the basket didn't seem nearly as interesting as what was inside it.

"I think you've been running and merely want to be caught," he said, leaning in close. "I'm very, very fast."

"I'm glad," she whispered.

"And I have the stamina for long chases. Though I'll warn you, most of my prey gives up pretty quickly."

"Are you planning to run me to ground, cowboy?" she asked, knowing in her heart that she'd waited too long for a man to make her feel the way Bandera did.

Before she could think twice, he kissed her, long and hard, his tongue searching, his lips possessing hers with fierce urgency. Holly gasped, feeling magic and a storm of longing rising inside her.

He was hot and hard and muscular—and they were in the balloon of her dreams. "I think you represent the change I want in my life," she said breathlessly.

He smiled. "I intend to change your life completely."

Could she throw a lifetime of planning to the wind? He was fabulous and sexy. This was the hot emotion she'd been hoping for in her marriage—she now knew it would have been lacking with Chuck.

"I'm glad I didn't get married," she said, pulling Bandera closer. It was wonderful to be floating in a beautiful balloon with a man who made her feel as if the worst part of her heartbreak had been swept away.

He kissed her again sweetly, not wanting to let her go. "You're amazing, Holly." He hugged her to him, thinking that he didn't want to give her up, no matter what.

She was his now.

And just as that thought sent terror rushing

through him, the balloon made a long, ripping sound above their heads. Holly gasped, clutching Bandera as they both fell backward from the force of the crash. They waited for more disaster, and Holly squeezed her eyes shut as she lay against Bandera's chest.

"We hit a tree," Bandera said. "We were losing altitude."

She opened her eyes. "Because we didn't know how to keep the balloon in the air."

They glanced up into the balloon, which didn't look to be folding in on itself yet. But it was only a matter of time.

"Come on," Bandera said. "Let's at least get out of the tree. I'll bet the balloon's owner followed us in his vehicle and isn't far behind."

"I read about that once," Holly said, climbing over the edge and grabbing on to a tree limb. "Chase vehicles. Teams that are part of the balloon crew."

Bandera stared at the ground. "Goodbye, sanity."

Holly gasped as he jumped down. "Bandera!"

"Don't worry." He straightened, dusting off his jeans and putting his hat back on his head. "You learn about jumping from second-story bedrooms when you grow up on a ranch."

"Oh?" She narrowed her eyes as she maneuvered closer to the tree trunk. "Visit many girls on the second floor?"

"Nah. But if you want to visit girls, you have to

learn to jump out your own window. Mason was hell on curfew."

She'd bet Bandera knew several convenient methods of escape, himself. "I thought you were afraid of heights."

"Not when the risks are worth it." He grinned up at her. "And you were worth it. Now, don't get snippy. Shimmy on down here and let me catch an armful of that booty."

She glared at him. "Somehow my adventure has turned into your adventure."

"That's probably the way it should work in any good adventure. Shared risk. Congruent excitement."

He was annoying. He'd gotten very confident since he'd taken control of his fears—and hers. She made her way down the opposite side of the tree and then jumped to the ground so he couldn't grab her. "I don't need your help, thanks."

Bandera laughed. "Your coach awaits," he said, pointing to the truck, which pulled up fifty feet away.

"I think I'll stay and watch the men wrestle this thing down." She looked up into the tree. "It's not going to be easy."

"Hello!" the balloon's owner yelled as he ran toward them. "Are you all right?"

"We're fine. Don't worry," Bandera said.

"That's never happened before!" The poor man was so distressed that Holly felt sorry for him.

"We are fine," she assured him. "And I think your balloon may be in decent shape."

He looked at Bandera. "I do apologize. Somehow it came unmoored and off you went."

"It was okay," Bandera assured him.

"I promised her that my ride was safe as a baby's crib. She said you had a fear of unpredictability. Risk taking. Mind you, you didn't go very high, and you floated along slowly, but it must have seemed quite frightening to you and—"

"It's all right," Bandera said, his voice a growl. "Neither one of us is hurt."

So she thought she had to take care of him like a child! Protect him from his fears! He glared at Holly.

He should have known getting involved with a runaway bride was a bad idea.

"What?" she asked.

"The riskiest thing I've ever done, I just did with you," he said as the owner went around the tree to figure out how to rescue his balloon. "The flight was a trip, but kissing you…" He took a deep breath. "Come on, let's get out of here." He didn't want to think about just how shaken he was. And not because of the crash, either.

BANDERA NOW REALIZED he must have lost his mind. Somewhere over the tops of the trees, he'd forgotten who he was, who she was and what his mission was.

Holly was seducing him, plain and simple. And
he'd been going along for the ride, led by his libido
in the same tango that had ensnared his brothers.
Chase, capture, then become the captured.

This was where his dance ended, he vowed.

He and Holly were both a bit sunburned, but the
balloon was safe with its owner, who had driven them
back to Bandera's truck amid more apologies.

It was time to hit the road and keep heading in the
direction he should have been going before he got
sidetracked. He dialed his cell phone. "Mason!" he
barked, when his brother answered.

"Yeah?"

"Where the hell are you?"

Bandera refused to look Holly's way, though she
watched him as he drove.

She twitched the map. They hadn't followed one
line on that map, thanks to her!

"At Hawk's," Mason said. "Where the hell are *you?*"

"I'm…on the road."

"You should have been here hours ago."

Bandera sighed. "Long story. Has to do with chocolate chip cookies and hot air balloons."

"Well, quit fiddling around and let's get on with
it! I didn't know you were going to be such a drag
on my schedule. I can't be gone forever, you know.
Marielle has to get back home to her cat."

Mason's irritation made Bandera tense. He

couldn't be any more annoyed with the tiny blonde next to him if he tried. She had caught him up in her runaway scheme. Up in that balloon, she'd looked at him with those big eyes, her hands in his back jeans pockets, and he'd realized he was losing something—could it be his heart?—that he wasn't ready to give up.

"Tell Marielle her cat was happy as a cat can be when we left. And her chocolate chip cookies were delicious. I'll be there as soon as I can. No more detours are in the itinerary." He turned off his phone and dropped it onto the seat beside him.

Holly looked out the opposite window silently. He could tell she was hurt by his comments.

Okay, maybe he was being a bit of an ass. She'd had her dream day turn distinctly undreamy. Maybe she was just rebounding, and he'd provided the bound. Like she'd said, she'd wanted to kiss a cowboy.

He'd been standing there, his body more ready than his mind, to give her what she craved.

But then her craving had turned into his craving. Now he knew what she felt like. What she tasted like. It was going to take superhuman strength to stop the dance now, when he dearly wanted to keep knowing how she felt. Tasted.

He got more tense just thinking about what he wouldn't be able to discover. He had to remember it wasn't up to him to do anything more than give her a ride.

"From now on, we stay in the truck," he said sternly. "Until we get to my destination. From there, Cousin Mike takes you wherever your heart desires."

"Fine," she said coolly. "I've got an idea of what my heart *does* desire."

That caught his attention. He'd expected a protest. Perhaps he'd *hoped* she'd protest. "You are welcome to share."

"I'm ready to go back home."

He blinked. "Home?"

"Yes. I've had my fun. I should be with my parents now. It was selfish of me to leave them."

It was selfish of her to leave *him!* After their balloon ride, shouldn't she be trying to stick to him like glue?

No, that wasn't right. He was trying to *end* this dance. She should go back home, and he shouldn't care.

"Fine," he said, his voice rougher than he meant it to be. "We're not far from Hawk's."

"Hawk's?" She perked up. "That's a catchy name."

Jealousy bit at him, deep and hard, which he told himself was ridiculous. He'd never been jealous in his life! *And I'm not going to start now.* "Maybe I should take you back now, since you're in such a hurry."

"I'm fine," she said. Then she put her hand on the back of his neck, lightly massaging his corded muscles. The sensation of wanting to relax beneath her fingers was intense.

"Are you all right?" she asked. "Your eyebrows are knitted together, and your jaw is locked."

"I'm very well. Thank you for your concern."

"Are you sure? Because you look distinctly uncom—"

"This is my driving face," he said.

"Maybe I should drive," she suggested. "And let your inner being flow to a more relaxed plane."

He wasn't going to relax, not with her in the truck and her fingers on his neck. "I just need to get you home."

She pulled her fingers away from his skin, which he regretted, and she went back to studying that infernal map. "I'll let you drive," he said suddenly. "I need a beer."

"Okay. Though you didn't strike me as the kind of man who would turn his truck keys over to a woman." She smiled at him. "I'm impressed by your lack of machismo."

He ignored that, because he hadn't realized there was anything symbolic about giving up his keys. Now that he knew there was, he was tempted to skip the beer.

Then again, if she drove, he could keep an eye on her better—surreptitiously, of course. He was getting a crick in his neck from bouncing his gaze between the road and the passenger seat. Holly was worth looking at, he admitted as he pulled to the shoulder. Even if it meant giving up his keys, which she took with a foxy wink.

Oh, boy. "There is no hidden subtext in you driving my vehicle," he said. "Stop trying to alarm me."

"I'm a very safe driver," she told him. "You just sit back and relax."

His cell phone rang, so he switched it on, keeping one eye on the blonde getting behind the wheel. "Hey, Mimi."

He stood beside the driver's-side door, his gaze on Holly as she checked out the seat positioning. Maybe he wouldn't shut the door just yet. He liked watching her move around, settling her fanny just so. "Um, Mason's not with me."

Holly glanced at him, her brows raised.

"Well… I don't know why you can't reach him," Bandera said. "Maybe he's out of range. In a bad cell area or something." He blinked. "Um, okay, Mimi. I should be catching up to him soon. I'll tell him."

Holly's gaze was sympathetic, but encouraging, too. Encouraging him to be honest.

But he couldn't tell Mimi the truth. There was too much history between Mimi and Mason. It shouldn't matter to either of them what the other one did, but it did matter somehow. To both of them. Bandera had seen that in the stubborn set of his brother's jaw.

He switched off the phone.

Holly looked at him curiously.

"Family stuff." He shrugged.

"I take it your brother might not have belonged on that bike with—"

"One can never say in my family. Very complicated, and not always understandable."

"Families are like that."

"Really." He figured no family was quite as unhinged as his. "We have good hearts. Just not always the wisdom we should." Closing the door, he walked around the truck, grabbing a beer out of the cooler as he went. "Want something? There are beverages in here besides beer."

"I'm fine." She started the truck, gunning it a little bit. "Are you sure you shouldn't have grabbed two of those for yourself?"

Her wink riled him. "Lady, I can handle anything you've got."

They stared at each other. Her eyes were wide and unblinking, and startled.

"I didn't mean that exactly the way it sounded," he said, worried that he might have tossed out a challenge that didn't seem very gentlemanly.

"That's too bad," she said. "There for a moment, I thought you might be the man of my dreams."

Chapter Five

Well, Holly was mistaken, Bandera thought irritably. He would never be the man of any woman's dreams.

"I'm going to nap," he said, aware that his tone was surly. "Follow the map, and try not to engage in any mishaps. Tell me when we get where we're going."

"Maybe we should go back the way we came."

He hesitated. "That doesn't sound right. One should never go backward. Only forward. I want to go forward to find Mason. You want to go forward to find yourself."

"No," Holly said, "I don't need to find myself. I already know who and what I am. Don't confuse me with my almost-marriage. I nearly married a man who didn't know who he was, though he saved me by skipping out on me."

Bandera grunted. "I see nothing heroic in your ex's actions."

"Well, that's you. I'm merely grateful. I am an optimist."

That was clear to see. The woman had optimistic written all over her. "I shouldn't ask this, but why do you not see me as the man of your dreams anymore?"

"Oh. You obviously haven't figured yourself out yet. I need someone stable." She smiled at him kindly, as if she were speaking to a less intelligent being. "Two stable people make a stable life together. You see how much trouble Mimi and Mason are having. One of them isn't stable."

"Mason," he said with a growl. "Though we always thought it was Mimi."

Holly nodded wisely. "I suspect instability of some nature runs in your family."

"It doesn't!" he protested—then drew a deep breath. Of course it did. He and his brothers were a manic table of numbers that couldn't be graphed. Random elements preferring the unknown.

"Even if we do have some moments—like every normal family—that aren't quite stable, it doesn't mean we're not a good family."

"Of course not. It just means one or more of you don't know who you are."

This girl was really starting to bug him. "Yeah, well." Bandera took a swig of his beer. "A little instability, indecisiveness and unexplained randomness is good for you."

"You're worried, aren't you?"

"About what?" He looked at her from under his hat, trying to disguise the fact that he admired the way she was handling the truck.

"You're worried you're going to end up like your brother Mason. Caught in a weird life."

"No," he lied.

"I think I am 'the weird' for you. You kissed *me* first, you know. But I want you to know you don't have anything to worry about. I'm not looking for a man."

Bandera turned his face to the window. "You should. You're a nice girl. You have lots of spunk. I like spunk in a woman."

"I wouldn't have guessed that." She reached over and patted his hand. "But it's okay. You've been very kind to give me a ride. And I like you thinking you're going to show me another side of life."

"Did I say that?"

"Yes. You said you would expose me to randomness and some other nonsense, which you apparently feel I need. I'm willing." She smiled at him. "What girl wouldn't want to ride with a sexy cowboy? I should be at home with my parents, and yet here I am with you. I have a lot in common with Mason, riding away from my obligations."

Bandera sat up. "You're making me nervous."

She laughed.

"Look, if we're going to be traveling buddies, you have to not do that."

"Do what?" she asked.

"Talk in circles. You have to settle down. A man can take only so much of that stuff."

She removed her hand from his, smiling. "You're all right, for an anal-retentive cowboy. Tough on the outside, pillowy soft around the heart."

He scowled. "Holly, you are baiting the wrong bull."

But she was right. He was enjoying having her around. Even if it alarmed him that she thought she knew him.

"It's okay," she said. "I know I'm safe with you."

"No, you're not." He thought about that for a few seconds, remembering their time in the balloon. "Although I'm not certain why you're not safe. I think it has to do with your lips."

"My lips?"

"Yeah. They fit mine very well. I think that's a bad sign. You're definitely not safe."

"Oh." She looked at him for a second. "Well, maybe they didn't fit as good as you remembered."

He thought they probably fit better. "Pull over."

"Here?"

"Just to the shoulder. Put on the hazard lights."

"I hardly think it's needed. We're the only car I've seen in probably ten minutes." But she flipped the flashing lights on, stopping the truck on the shoulder. "Now what?"

"Kiss me."

She blinked. "You had me pull over so you could command a kiss?"

"Yes." He pointed to her lips. "I want to know if those—" he touched a finger gently to the soft velvet of her mouth "—are as matched to mine as I thought they were."

"There's no such thing as matching mouths," she protested. "People are not puzzles."

"You are and I am, and these are the pieces that may or may not fit."

It was all nonsense, but he had to know, Bandera thought, bringing her to him with strong hands. His lips touched hers, then claimed them—but the best part was she kissed him back.

Nothing had ever felt better in his life. "You're scaring me real bad," he said huskily before kissing her faster, harder. "And I don't scare easy."

"I don't understand," she said, closing her eyes as he kissed her mouth, her chin, her neck.

"You fit me," he said, "and yet you nearly married a poor excuse of a man. You should be ashamed."

"But he asked, and I thought I loved him." She pulled back slightly to look at Bandera. "Even if I loved you, you would never ask."

He didn't want to go into what he would or

wouldn't do, so he touched the sequins on her pretty top. "Never say yes to someone who isn't a perfect fit."

"I never said yes at all. Except to the marriage proposal," she said, her eyes lustrous in the waning light.

"You would say yes to me."

She laughed. "You keep thinking that, cowboy." Flipping off the hazard lights, she pulled back onto the road. "Saying no kept me out of a lot of trouble. What if I'd say yes and become pregnant?"

She stared at him, no longer smiling, before looking fixedly back at the road.

"Well, you and I wouldn't be kissing," he said matter-of-factly. "But suppose you met The One. And you let yourself get all bugged out. You'd be too nervous to say yes and then he'd go off on his white steed and you'd have missed the handsome prince."

She thought about that. "I thought I had The One. And now I'm kissing you." She flipped the radio to a country and western station, sighing. "I chose Bach and Handel for my wedding music."

"That was your first mistake. What's wrong with Willie?"

She turned her head to stare at him. "Willie Nelson for a wedding march?"

"Or at least a groom-warmer."

"Groom-warmer?"

"Well, they probably pipe some kind of music in

to keep the groom calm. I'd want Willie. Waylon. And the boys."

She groaned. "My wedding was going to be very elegant."

"And yet it got messy. That's because you didn't plan it right, with the correct groom. Was Chuck a cowboy?"

"No."

"Ever ridden a horse?"

"No."

"Did you have a piñata in the backyard for the kiddies to swing at?"

"At a wedding?" Holly asked.

"And were the guests drinking beer and wine, or those fancy things with plastic swords floating around in them, usually piercing an olive as big as a golf ball? I want more beverage and less plastic decorations in my cup."

She smiled. "We were serving wine, mainly. Champagne, water, tea."

"Was there a petting zoo for the children?"

"It was a *wedding,* Bandera."

"Well, at least a pony for pony rides," he amended.

"Look," she said, "you seem awfully fixated on children. Do you have any?"

"No," he said thoughtfully, staring at his beer bottle, "but I'm getting real envious of my brothers who do."

"Why?"

"I don't know. I just realized it as we were strategizing about what went wrong with your wedding."

"The only thing that went wrong was the groom."

"No, the planning was all wrong. It was too sterile."

"Elegant."

"It lacked pizzazz and fire. Smokin' hot lads and passionate smart ladies." He sighed. "You're hung up on the wrong things in life."

She waved a hand at him. "Go on. I'm dying to hear."

"A woman makes a man feel like a man by noticing how he looks, even when he's wearing his boxers and reading the newspaper in bed. She tells him he's handsome and she gets him a cup of coffee. In public, she holds his arm and occasionally smiles sweetly up at him. This can be the best part of a man's day."

Holly blinked, and he saw a frown begin to gather between her brows. It made him smile. Baiting her was so easy.

"That sounds so…chauvinistic," she protested.

"But I like it," he said. "Go ahead. Try it."

"No, thank you."

He laughed, pushing his hat down over his face and leaning back to relax. "Wake me when you get to Wichita. We'll need to turn around there."

"Turn around? You're not making me drive all the way there just to turn around while you sleep!"

"Turn around there," he said slowly. "Somewhere around there, we'll need to get on the road to Hawk's."

"Oh. Well, why don't you speak more clearly?"

"I've been trying," he said. "It seems we don't fit together anywhere but our lips."

AND THAT WAS THAT, Holly realized as he dozed off. As a wedding planner, she'd recoiled from everything he'd suggested for such an event. The way he saw his nuptials wasn't her kind of happily-ever-after.

Willie, Waylon and the boys? She shivered. No woman wanted that.

She'd wanted the traditional fairy tale, complete with white gown and moon-white roses. The dream come true. "I tried too hard," she muttered.

"S'okay," he muttered in his sleep.

She sighed. It wasn't okay. She was going to have to grow and change if she wasn't going to make more dumb mistakes in her life. "Wedding planning is not my forte," she said. "I'm going to change my life."

"S'okay," he repeated.

She wanted to reach over and smack him out of his peaceful snoozing. It was not okay to discover that everything you thought was, wasn't.

Funny how this cowboy was making her old life seem so predictable—and maybe just a bit empty.

"It's not okay, and I can't dream those dreams any longer," she said, but this time he didn't answer.

MIMI TOOK A DEEP BREATH as she stared at the phone. Bandera had been uncomfortable. She knew the Jeffersons too well. There were very few secrets between people who had grown up together. And he'd definitely been unwilling to get into a long conversation about Mason's whereabouts.

From Last, Mimi had learned that Mason was on another road trip to find out about his past. She understood his drive. Much of her behavior today was influenced by her mom, who'd chosen a search for the bright lights of Hollywood over being married to a small-town sheriff and raising a daughter.

Mimi intended to be a very different kind of mother. She looked at her daughter, smiling as she slept in her new bed. When they'd made the move away from the ranch to the small town house in Union Junction, Mimi had bought Nanette a big-girl bed. Mason had hauled it to the house and put it together for her. Lovingly, the two of them had made the bed, with Nanette dancing around excitedly. Mason had painted the walls of Nanette's room a soft shell-pink, and he'd laid on the bed pretty unicorn pillows he'd ordered from a catalog.

Mimi's eyes had teared up as the three of them ate dinner that night. And she'd come to a realization: it was time to be that very different mother she wanted so much to be. A good mother. A loving mother.

A mother who cared enough to be strong for her daughter.

She sat down on her daughter's bed, gently touching her child's face. Why had she never been able to tell Mason how she felt about him? Because they were more comfortable being best friends rather than dealing with what she really felt for him.

But avoiding her feelings was what had gotten her to this moment, she knew. She had never wanted to lose Mason—what she had of him—and so she'd hidden her true emotions. "When your grandfather got so sick and nearly died," she whispered to her daughter, "I married a man Dad liked and trusted so he could see me happy. I desperately wanted to give him a grandchild." Gently, she touched the blond strands of hair that curled around her daughter's ear. "I wouldn't change a thing I did. And maybe that's wrong. But you," she said softly, "you are the angel my heart dreamed of. And you're *his* angel, too. Mason loves you so much."

Tears stung her eyes, tears of regret and false hope. When she'd married Brian and ran away from her broken heart, a heart that loved but was not loved in return, she'd only hoped to make her father happy.

Life had a way of making the repercussions of some decisions linger a long time.

Now her father was almost fully recovered from a liver ailment he had not been expected to survive. The doctors said that her loving care had probably turned the tide during the nearly three and a half years it had attacked him. He would never be the strong, tough-as-bricks sheriff he'd been, but neither was he an invalid at death's door. Now that they'd moved to town, and Mimi had run for sheriff herself, he had a ton of visitors coming in, mostly older gentlemen wanting a game of checkers or a bit of gossip or a chat about the old days. An occasional widow came by, too, bearing sweets she'd baked for him.

Her dad loved being the center of attention. Before his illness, he'd always been too busy with the ranch and his job to enjoy life.

Nanette murmured in her sleep, a contented snuffle as she changed her breathing pattern. Mason liked to hold her and read her to sleep. A lot of Winnie-the-Pooh, which Nanette insisted on, and then Mason would read some outdated classical Greek philosopher or even a Bible story. It depended upon his mood. By then, Nanette had had her Winnie, and she was in Mason's arms, and she didn't care what Euclidian, Pythagorean, or biblical construct Uncle Mason was trying to introduce her to.

She did like the stories of the angels, though. The philosophers and mathematicians she ignored.

It had been a glimpse into Mason's life that Mimi

could only marvel at. Maverick Jefferson had done an amazing job of educating his children. The Jeffersons had attended public school with her, but it had mainly been a social exercise for them. It was Maverick who'd shaped those boys intellectually.

She could understand Mason's desire to find out what had happened to their father. She put her finger in Nanette's hand, and her daughter tightened her fist around it. Nanette would someday want to know about *her* father.

This had become very clear to Mimi one day in the bakery. Several little girls had come after church to get cookies and doughnuts, all with their fathers in tow. Nanette had stood on uncertain feet, her smile wide as she watched the families enter, a crumbling cookie in her hand as everybody walked in and made much of her.

One day, she would ask about her father. Would he attend church with her? Would he go to the bakery afterward? Would he…would he…

Mimi's heart tore. There was so much she'd been afraid to say.

But then Mason had left before she could tell him her feelings.

She stood, turning out the tiny lamp beside Nanette's bed. It wasn't too late to say what needed to be said. It was, however, too late to continue being afraid of losing Mason.

Whatever happened, whether they remained friends or became something more, was less important than Nanette growing up knowing what was right and wrong and knowing the truth about her world.

Mimi picked up her overnight bag, knowing Nanette was in good hands with Grandpa and the myriad "aunts and uncles" who liked to come visit. Mimi wouldn't be gone long.

Just long enough to finally put the past to rest.

BANDERA AND HOLLY CAUGHT up with Mason, Marielle, Cousin Mike and Hawk in the arroyo. It wasn't, Bandera mused, exactly the way he'd meant to introduce Holly to the tracker, but apparently, Hawk liked to hold his gatherings among Indian totems, near a cave hidden behind large, spiky bushes.

"Sheesh, Hawk," he said. "We might never have found this place if you hadn't told us where to look."

"Who's this?" Hawk demanded.

"Holly. She's…finding herself."

Hawk grunted. Holly held out her hand. "It's nice to meet you," she said.

Hawk shook her hand briefly, then turned back around to look at Mason. "Dude, did you have to bring a whole brigade with you?"

"It didn't start out that way," Mason said wryly. "When I left this morning, it was just me." He sent a glare toward Bandera, but his brother just shrugged.

"This is where Ranger married Hannah," Hawk said. "I performed the ceremony."

"Really?" Holly's eyes glowed, the wedding planner in her coming alive, Bandera supposed. "Kind of hard to get the wedding party in here."

Hawk grimaced. "The wedding party rolled down the hill into the arroyo, after stepping on a poisonous plant. The howl could be heard for miles."

Holly blinked. Bandera hid a smile. "This isn't really the right spot to think about planning a wedding," he told her.

"Oh, I'm not," she said. "I'm not planning weddings anymore. I've decided upon a new business."

"You have?" Bandera said. "Already?"

"Yes. I'm going to open the Honeymoon Balloons company, complete with hot air balloon, secluded cabin and lavish food service. Very secluded. Very romantic. Think bed-and-breakfast in the air."

He stared at her. "You are nuts."

"Ahem." Hawk cleared his throat. "Mason has something on his mind."

They all sat on rocks in the canyon. Holly perched as far away from Bandera as possible, he noticed, probably annoyed at his lack of support for her business idea. But how was a man supposed to react to such a crazy idea?

Then again, he thought, *I'm sitting in a canyon with a medicine man, a couple of perfect strangers and a runaway bride.* What was normal about that?

Holly shifted on her rock, staring at Mason as he spoke. Bandera barely listened as his brother outlined his proposal to Hawk. Bandera was concentrating on Holly's pursed lips. Maybe she wasn't pursing, he thought. They were just naturally plump and kissable and inviting—

"Bandera," Hawk said, his tone annoyed. "Are you with us?"

"With who?" he asked, snapped from his musings.

"With me and Mason. I'm heading to Alaska to look for information on your father. Cousin Mike is going to escort Marielle back home, and Holly is…"

His voice trailed off.

"I'm fine," Holly said brightly. "I was planning on riding with my cousin, anyway. I can go back home with him. I want to stop at that balloon festival and ask some questions."

Marielle perked up. "I've got some land near my motorcycle shop you could rent from me, which would be perfect for that type of getaway."

Holly beamed. "I'll go with you, then. Thanks."

Something nettled Bandera's heart. The woman was so independent. It was annoying! Women who were interested in a man, who returned their interest, usually tried to hang around. In fact, any woman he had ever kissed usually did her darnedest to stay very close to him.

Holly seemed determined to run away. He supposed it was in her blood, just as some Jefferson things were in his own blood. Clearly, her motivation and his were not meant to mix.

"Bandera?" Hawk asked. "What are you going to do?"

"If I don't go with Mason," Bandera said with a sigh, "he may never return home. That's my job, following Mason back to Union Junction."

Marielle laughed. "He doesn't seem like such a bad boy to me."

Mason blushed, Bandera noted with interest.

When everyone had made their plans, Bandera stared at Holly. She raised her chin, looking right back at him stubbornly.

"You'll regret stopping your run so soon," he said softly.

"You'll have regrets, too," she replied, her eyes wide. "Mason can take care of himself."

"You don't know Mason," Bandera said. "Actually, none of my family takes care of themselves very well."

She laughed, turning toward Cousin Mike's motorcycle, but Bandera caught her hand. "You want to ride back in the truck and tell me more about this Honeymoon Balloon thing? I'm pretty sure you need me to brainstorm ideas with you."

"I do not," Holly said, removing her hand.

"Oh, go with him," Cousin Mike said suddenly, with a surreptitious look at Marielle. "He won't bite, and there's no rush to get back. Your mom called before you got here and said she and your dad are going on vacation."

She blinked. "Where?"

He shrugged. "I don't know. You'd gotten them so excited with your wedding and honeymoon plans that they decided to take one of their own. Think they murmured something about renewing their vows."

"Oh," Holly said softly, then smiled. "How very romantic of them."

"Yeah." Mike crossed his arms over his chest, glancing at Marielle. "Think it was on their minds."

Marielle blushed.

Mason's cell phone rang. He jumped, pulling it from his pocket.

"Hello? Hey, Mimi," he said.

The whole group stared at him.

"You are? Okay. Let me have Hawk tell you how to get to Jellyfish's then. There's no point in you stopping here, and we're on our way there." He passed the cell phone to Hawk. "Mimi's passing near here on her way to…to somewhere." He wrinkled his face. "I don't think she said where."

Hawk took the cell phone and gave her instructions.

"That reminds me," Bandera said, "Mimi called earlier. I meant to tell you."

"What did she want?"

She'd want you to not be with another woman, Bandera thought but didn't say. "I'm not sure. I told her I'd have you call her."

Holly looked at him funny. Okay, so he was prevaricating, but he didn't want to be caught in the middle of a Mimi-Mason miscommunication. Holly had no idea how tense things could get between those two.

"Okay." Mason turned away. "Thanks for the ride, Marielle."

"Anytime." She grinned up at him. "It was great riding with you. You know how to lean into the turns just right, cowboy."

Mason grinned back. "And you know all the right things to say to make a man feel good."

They kissed goodbye—on the cheek, Bandera noticed with some relief—then Mason headed to the truck. To the passenger seat. That meant Bandera was driving, and if Holly went with them she would be in the back seat. Alone. He did some quick seat rearranging in his mind. Before Mason was halfway to the truck, Bandera said, "You drive, Mason."

His brother caught the keys he tossed him. "Why?"

"So Holly's not alone in the back."

Marielle and Cousin Mike laughed. Holly glared. "I don't mind being alone in the back. I was planning on taking a nap. And changing out of this tank top. All these seed pearls and sequins are starting to bother me. I want to put on a comfy T-shirt."

Bandera's eyes went huge. Holly was planning on taking her shirt off in the truck. The thought was almost more than he could bear. His mouth dried out but his body began to sweat in strange places. Small, perky little breasts with nothing more than a bra covering them—

"Bandera," Mason said sternly. "Stop leering."

"I'm not leering!" Bandera glared at his brother. "For cripe's sake, Mason!"

"Well, whatever." Mason scratched his jaw. "Holly, I apologize for my brother's behavior. He can be a bit of an oaf."

"I'm not an oaf!" Bandera was on the verge of being really mad with his eldest brother. "You know, you're not the father figure in our house anymore, Mason, if you haven't noticed. We're all grown up, with our own wishes and responsibilities, and you don't have the right to shepherd us any longer."

Silence grew in the canyon as everyone went still. Overhead, the sun was covered by a cloud, and a hawk circled in the sky to the east. Somewhere a bird screeched and Bandera's heart did, too, because Holly was staring at him, shocked. As if she'd never seen him before.

Maybe she hadn't. Not the real him. Better she figure out just how malfunctioning their whole tribe was before she decided to go another mile with him.

"I'm just going to go sit in the truck," she said softly, "in the back, by myself, just me and my little purse and my Honeymoon Balloon retreat ideas."

Bandera glared at Mason, then turned on his heel and followed her to the truck. Silently, they both got in, she in the back and he in the front, while everyone else said goodbye to each other. Bandera stiffly avoided Holly, now that Mason had pointed out how he was acting. Maybe he was a sex-crazed oaf, but Mason didn't need to say that in front of her.

"Don't look," she said. "I'm going to do a quick change."

He swallowed hard. "I'm not turning around."

"Thank you."

He heard a pulling sound, like a zipper going down. He closed his eyes, not wanting to envision what he was envisioning. Skin, more skin, round breasts—

"It's stuck," Holly said. "Rats!"

"What's stuck?"

"The zipper. Don't turn around."

"I'm not!" Zippers weren't his department, other than the one on his jeans. He heard a ripping sound. "What was that?"

"I accidentally pulled too hard. But it's off," Holly said with a happy sigh. "I'm free from the silken prison."

He wasn't. "Are you dressed?"

"Yes. The feel of cotton is heaven. I never realized that before!"

"Well, you didn't plan on wearing a wedding gown for several hours."

"No, and I never will again. I'm skipping the whole concept next time."

He frowned. "Marriage or fancy gowns?"

"Both."

He wasn't certain he liked the sound of that. Not that marriage with Holly ever crossed his mind—it didn't, and it wouldn't—but she could at least be a little open to the possibility. "You'll probably be married by this time next year."

She laughed. "Bandera, you have no idea how great my desire is to avoid what I just ran away from."

Of their own accord his fingers drummed on the dash. "Actually, I do."

Sighing, she got out of the truck and went to the passenger side. "You drive, I'll sit here, we'll chat, and Mason can sit in the back and read the map."

Bandera perked up. "Why didn't I think of that?"

"I don't know. I think I confuse you."

Ignoring that, he closed her door for her, then went around to the driver's side. "Mason! Come on!" Getting in, he said, "Buckle up."

He leaned over to make sure her buckle was tight, pausing as he realized he'd gotten too close. She smelled good. He'd forgotten how much he liked being right up against her, feeling her soft, warm skin against his. His conscience kicked in, reminding him that today another man had meant to wed her, and all Bandera had done was kiss her rather tepidly, when he should have kissed her until she begged for—

No, no, that wasn't right. He *was* being an oaf! If he was any kind of gentleman, he'd remember that her heart was tender and delicate and today was her wedding day and he should leave her alone, and—

"Oh, forget it," he said, pulling her toward him. "Now that you've stripped off your last bit of wedding attire, let's celebrate." And he kissed her, rejoicing when he realized she was kissing him back without hesitation.

It felt great to be an oaf.

Mason cleared his throat as he got into the back of the truck. Bandera and Holly jumped apart nervously.

"Is that how they read maps nowadays?" Mason asked dryly. "Two heads are better than one—preferably locked at the—"

"Mason," Bandera said in warning.

"Sorry."

In the rearview mirror, Bandera could see Mason's grin. He wasn't sorry at all.

"I'm going to stretch out and nap," he said. "Let me know when Mimi catches up to us if I'm still asleep."

Bandera switched on some soft country music to prevent conversation. What had he been thinking, kissing Holly like that, out in the open where anybody could see them?

That's when he knew he was too close for comfort. Too close to losing his head. She tempted him. She made his body scream with questions he wanted answered.

It's just because she's safe, he told himself. After all, she'd made her case over and over again. She intended to stay single. The whole wedding thing had gotten her down. She'd even decided to change her business.

So that meant he must just be taking advantage of her weak moment. Which was unchivalrous as hell.

He vowed not to touch her again.

Her fingers touched his wrist. He glanced up, seeing the smile that gently lit her face. "It's okay," she said. "I liked it."

Maybe she had, but she didn't know what she was talking about. People with damaged hearts rarely did. All his life he'd been surrounded by humans with banged up hearts who acted irrationally. He knew exactly what happened when the ol' love bug got squashed on your windshield.

In the back seat, Mason snored, not a bit worried, it seemed, that the woman who'd squashed his heart like a bug was on the way to see him.

Maybe, Bandera thought, *I'm taking this all too seriously.* He pulled his hand away from Holly's and moved the truck into gear, heading down the road.

"It won't work," he said. "It's all wrong."

"That's okay," she said. "I'm okay with wrong. I already tried right, and it didn't feel anywhere near as good as this does."

He ground his teeth. No woman could snap back as fast as Holly had. But he wanted so badly to believe that neither her wedding nor her groom had meant a thing to her.

She said she hadn't loved the guy, but still…she might be trying to save face. Or convince herself. She *had* to be terribly hurt.

Yet Bandera wanted her, and he wanted to push away all the bad memories of her destroyed wedding day so that she'd move forward thinking only of him.

"I've decided you protest too much," he said suddenly. "Marry *me*. I'll treat you so good you'll think every day is your wedding day."

Chapter Six

Holly stared at Bandera, shocked by his proposal. Was he serious? He seemed serious…but one could never tell with a man, and probably even less with one of these wily Jeffersons. "I don't think so," she said. "We're just passing the time by kissing each other."

"Yes, but together we'd run an excellent bed-and-breakfast. As long as you didn't spend all your time floating around in a hot air balloon."

"You want to go into business with me?" she asked. "I'm not too crazy about that idea. You're a bit bossy, and I was sort of looking forward to being on my own."

"Yes, but how can we run an effective honeymoon business unless we're married? We need to show that we know what we're talking about."

She blinked. "Are you making a business proposal or a marriage proposal?"

"Both. I believe one sweetens the other."

She shook her head, wondering what the man was really up to. "Besides the fact that we like kissing each other, what's the catch? What's in it for you?"

He jerked his head toward the back seat. "I get away from the family."

"You could move to Montana and achieve that."

He met her statement with a shrug. "And I could marry you."

"You don't know me. You don't love me."

"Judging by the fact that you left your wedding to hang out by the road with a big sign, there are different levels of love. Maybe it's best to grow into these things."

"We're totally opposite," she said.

"I like contrary things. I'm used to them."

"But you didn't want to get married just thirty minutes ago."

"True," he conceded. "But I would like to make love to you, and the only way that's going to happen is if you're married. That's what you told loverboy, and I believe you."

She hesitated. "You would marry me just to make love to me?"

"Well, that's not the only reason. It's just the best reason I can think of."

"It's so male chauvinist. Or maybe male opportunist."

He laughed. "Probably. But I would be stupid not

to tell you that you're sexy. And a wedding ring suddenly doesn't seem like that big of a drawback if I get to kiss your lips every night."

"I can't marry you," she said. "Even if I believed you were serious, which I don't, I'm not about to take you away from your search for your father."

"Oh." Bandera frowned. "Listen, that trail is cold. Even Hawk won't be able to figure this out. Dad left. His heart cracked, and maybe he lost his mind. We'll never know. But he's long, long gone." He sighed. "By now, passed away, I'm sure. Mason knows it. Truthfully, I think if he and Mimi could have settled down and made a go of it, he wouldn't have this urge to find out what happened to Dad."

"His quest seems pretty reasonable to me."

"Yeah, well. Hang around us a little while longer and you'll begin to question everything you ever thought was reasonable."

She turned to glance at Mason, who was deeply asleep, clearly taking advantage of the time to relax. Crossing a leg underneath her and hoping to avoid the subject of families and matrimony, she said, "How did you get the name Bandera?"

"Bandera's Pass," he said. "Long story."

"Where are we going?" she asked curiously. "If it's far, you may have time to tell me."

"We are going to the land of Jellyfish," he said quixotically, "and we're not far away."

"It's not necessary to be totally mysterious, Bandera. You know my secrets. I can know some of yours. How can we get married if you don't share?" She tapped his forearm lightly, marveling at how strong his muscles were under his skin. How well-formed and rough-hewn this man was.

"Ah, so you're considering my proposal?"

"No," she said bluntly. "Neither business nor otherwise. I'm just exploiting your proposal. You don't really want a wife. You're just running away."

"I'm running away?" He turned to stare at her. "That doesn't seem fair, coming from you."

She sighed. "Bandera's Pass, please."

He looked back at the road. "Well, all the boys were named after something in Texas. Usually a city or historical event. I was named after the incident at Bandera's Pass."

"Very melodramatic," she said. "I like it."

"Hey! How melodramatic is running from your own wedding? You could have confronted your groom at the altar, or called him, or had the minister intercede, but no." He glared at her. "You skipped out, missy. Don't tell me about melodramatic."

"Sensitive." She patted his hand. "It's kind of sexy on you."

"Well." He looked embarrassed. "I think everything about you is sexy. So sexy, in fact, that I have the same urge I used to get as a child chasing after fireflies. I wanted to catch them and put them in a bottle."

She gasped, her heart speeding up. "You know, there are times when I can't decide if you're romantic or crazy. You can't tell a woman you want to catch her and put her in a bottle!"

He laughed. "So much for sensitivity."

"Try *scary.*"

"No, it's just that you're all, you know, light. Fascinating. Firefly-like."

"Oh." What was she supposed to say to that? "Thank you."

He sighed happily. "You're welcome. There for a minute, I was afraid you might be offended by a compliment. Some women think a man is after something if he compliments her."

She laughed. "You *are* after something. You admitted it."

"Yeah. Fifty percent of your balloon business, partners straight down the middle. I think you're on to something with that. And I don't want you telling Jellyfish or he'll be on it like white on rice. He used to commandeer a floating palace."

The smile faded from her face. "You're offering financial backing?"

"Absolutely. I need a side business," he said thoughtfully. "And if Marielle's property is what you're looking for, you can be manager of the business, and I'll take care of the land and maintenance. Along with the financial backing."

What Bandera was offering was wonderful. It might mean she wouldn't have to go to a bank to describe her air-spun dream for a loan. There would be a man to help with the upkeep, no small thing for the business she was imagining. It would allow her to concentrate specifically on her customers' needs. One day, she might even be able to expand—

"I don't know," she said honestly. "I sort of like the idea of going it alone."

"No, you don't," he said. "You really want me on the team."

"Is this with marriage or without?" she asked, trying to keep her voice light, but wondering where he'd been going with his strange ideas. Strange, but somehow compelling.

"I don't believe in marriage," Mason said, stretching.

"We know," Bandera said, his tone dry.

Holly turned to look at Mason curiously. "Don't you want children?"

"Children!" Bandera smacked himself on the forehead. "Of course you'll want kids," he said to her.

Holly stiffened. "No less than two and no more than four," she said.

"Four." Mason whistled. "That's a lot of little people."

"You never want any children?" Holly repeated, wondering why Mason was avoiding her question. "Kids keep us young. They make us real."

"I don't know," he replied. "I'm not much of a kid person."

"The heck you're not," Bandera said. "You love Mimi's little girl."

"Yeah, well." Mason pushed his hat down low over his eyes and moved to position himself to fall asleep again.

"So what about you?" Holly asked Bandera.

"What about me?"

"Do you want to have children?"

He paused. "Honestly, only the practice of making babies has appealed to me heretofore. I never thought about any long-term commitment."

Mason snorted under his hat.

"Oh, well, you can snort," Bandera said. "You already have a little girl."

"He does?" Holly asked. She frowned at Mason in the back seat.

"Well, he has a little girl who adores him. It's Mimi's daughter. She thinks Mason is the only man on the planet, though the rest of us uncles try desperately to squeeze in for some attention."

"Oh." Holly smiled to herself. "My mom would like to have some grandbabies. She really thought this wedding was going to bring her the little ones she wants."

"Maybe it should just be a business commitment between us," Bandera said. "I really wasn't planning on having kids. You have to understand, I'm from a family of twelve boys, and they're all children."

From under his hat, Mason sighed deeply.

"And he's the biggest one of all," Bandera whispered.

"I'm sensing that." Holly looked at Bandera. "I don't know if I trust you to be a business partner. You're awfully random."

"But steadfast in ways you can only imagine. I only appear random on the surface. Deep inside, I'm a really steady guy."

Holly glanced over the back seat, waiting for another snort from Mason, but all she heard was silence. "Steady guy with no kids, huh?"

"That describes my goals," he said. "Since we're being honest, what are yours?"

She sighed. "All the ones I had for the past year changed today. Give me a little while to figure them out."

"Sorry. Unfair question." He reached over and took her hand in his. "I'll tell you a little secret."

"What?"

"I'm just joshing you about trying to get you into bed."

"You are?" Vague disappointment bloomed through her.

"Yeah. Listen. I've been trying to keep your mind off everything. I think you're taking it all very bravely, keeping a stiff upper lip and your feelings to yourself, which I understand."

He massaged her fingertips, which she liked and yet didn't, because it felt good, and she wasn't sure if she wanted him to make her feel good when he was talking about joshing her. She withdrew her fingers from his, opting for independence.

"Now, don't get your feelings hurt," he said with a wink. "You're a beautiful woman, and I can't stand to see beautiful women cry. I want you to smile, and I want you to try to forget the jerk you left behind many miles ago now."

"I may be trying to forget about the jerk driving this truck," Holly said crossly. "Has it ever occurred to you that maybe I didn't need your... peppiness?"

"Peppiness?" He frowned. "What's that?"

"A good humor man trying to ride in and save my emotions. You, Mr. Peppy."

He turned to look at her. "So you want to consider the physical benefits of our business model?" he asked with a grin.

"Cowboy, I only wanted a kiss from you, which I got, thank you very much." She laid her head against the truck window and closed her eyes. "Anything more would be overkill."

"You think?" he asked, sounding pretty proud of himself.

"Yes," she said with a sigh. "You couldn't handle catching this firefly."

"Yeah, but you'd go good in my bottle."

AN HOUR LATER, when she'd awakened from a nap and put on lip gloss, she hopped out to meet Jellyfish and Mimi. Holly couldn't tell which one she was most astounded by.

Jellyfish was huge, a big, handsome man who was clearly in tune with the earth and all the natural surroundings. She stared at him, wondering how he ever found clothes that fit.

And Mimi was beautiful in a very sweet, feminine way. Her gaze seemed to seek Mason often. He looked for her, too, in a protective yet wary way.

They were friends, Holly realized, but their friendship was also adrift for some reason.

"Hello," Bandera said, coming up behind her. "You look so serious. Regrets?"

"Only that I didn't slap you while we were in the truck," Holly said without rancor and just from a desire to pick at him. "Mimi's really pretty."

"I guess so," Bandera said, "in a little-sister way."

She blinked. "Bandera, she's a knockout."

"Well, don't be jealous," he said. "You're not exactly ugly."

"You're the backside of a donkey, Bandera," she said, heading away from him toward the creek, where Jellyfish's house sat hidden by a stand of leafy trees.

"Wait," he said, striding behind her to catch her hand and slow her down. "I like needling you as much as you like needling me. Only you don't seem to like it when you get needled. What's up with that?"

He had a point. "I don't know. Maybe your arrogance bothers me."

"I don't mean to be unfriendly," he said, surprising her. "My only goals are to run my ranch, read great poetry and maybe rescue a damsel or two."

"What am I supposed to do with that?" she demanded, putting her hands on her hips. "I'm not a damsel, but I'm presuming you think you rescued me."

"No," he said, pulling her closer to him, "you rescued me." He kissed her once, ever so softly, on the lips. "I could never put you in a jar. Your lips are so soft I'd hate to waste time taking the lid off."

"Bandera," she said, pulling away from him. "Do not kiss me."

"Okay," he said easily. "Suit yourself."

That annoyed her even more. He made it sound as though she were giving up something wonderful! Turning, she headed to the creek.

"Let's go canoeing," he suggested. "While Mason fills Jellyfish in on what he wants from the journey they're taking."

"I thought you were going, too."

"I might," he said, pulling the canoe off the embankment so they could ease it into the water. "Then again, it depends on how fast we get our honeymoon retreat idea going. I think we should go back to that man whose balloon we crashed and ask him to give us lessons in flying, first off. Secondly, he can give us pointers on running a business that includes hot air balloons."

She couldn't believe Bandera was so interested in her idea. Truthfully, it warmed her soul that he approved of it. She had to admit that her ex-fiancé had dismissed her creativity, suggesting that one day she would stop working to stay at home. While she wanted to be a mother and take care of her children, she hadn't thought giving up her business was such a good idea. She was good at making other people's dreams come true.

Just not her own.

"You really do think it's a good idea, don't you?"

He glanced up as he helped her into the canoe. "You sound so shocked. It's a helluva good idea." *Once I got to thinking about it.*

"It's just that I don't see you as being the kind of guy who is interested in wedding stuff."

"Shoot, as long as it's not my party, I'm all for it. I vote we keep a couple horses on the property, too, so that the guests can ride if they wish." He pushed away from shore with a paddle.

"Horses," she said softly. "That's a great idea."

"I'm full of them." He smiled at her, and her heart sang a disjointed tune. *He likes my idea, and he likes me,* she thought—and then realized she was happy because he believed in her.

But other than that—and their matching lips—they didn't have a whole lot in common.

"I'm confused," she said. "Is it me or my idea you're interested in?"

"Both," he said honestly, paddling lazily to the middle of the creek. "Now here's the trick. You have to close your eyes and relax for the thirty minutes we're out here. Not one word leaves those velvety pink lips of yours." He laid the paddle in the bottom of the boat, stretched out, leaned back and covered his face with his hat.

"What are you doing?"

"Shh," he said arrogantly. "No talking. Just unwind."

And that was that. Paddle down, hat over face, determined to relax. Holly sighed, glancing around for signs of danger, like a waterfall or rocks. Nothing except trees dotted the creek edge. An occasional fish bubbled at the water's surface, and the wonderful feel of late sunshine warmed her skin.

Slowly, she edged down into a reclining position, trying to mimic Bandera. Basically, that meant aligning her feet beside his hips. Frowning, she told herself that this was not too intimate a thing to do with a man she'd only met today. It was not romantic. He was not going to seduce her in the middle of this creek. He genuinely seemed interested in his nap.

"You'd probably be more comfortable if you lay against my chest," he said. "Not that I'm rushing you or anything."

She was about to say something to rebuke his obvious lure to temptation, but just as she opened her mouth a loud splash near the pier stopped her. Bandera sat up, swiping his hat off his face just in time to see Mimi walking to her truck as Mason swam toward shore.

Chapter Seven

Bandera sighed as he watched his brother hit the creek-bank and head off after Mimi. "You see how it is."

Holly nodded. "Crazy."

"Yeah." He wanted to lie back down in the boat and relax, but at this point he knew he was too tense to do it. No doubt Mason had gotten his just desserts, and Mimi was always willing to ladle out those desserts with an extra-large spoon. "He probably said something stupid."

"Like he didn't believe in marriage. I thought that was sort of unwise when he said it in the truck," Holly murmured.

"This from the bride on the run?"

"Would you stop saying that?" She stared at him crossly. "All parties concerned are happy with the way matters worked out."

"Even you."

"Well, I wouldn't be sitting in a canoe if matters

had gone as planned, which tells me that even the best wedding planners can't control every detail."

"There are always random occurrences." He thought about that for a moment. "As I said, I have always liked random."

"Would you like it in your wedding?"

"I don't know. There was a time, when Mimi got married and the minister asked if anybody had any objections…" He stopped and looked at Holly, knowing she'd probably not approve of what they'd done. "We actually took bets on whether Mason would stop the wedding or not."

She shrugged. "Why would he?"

"Because he cares about Mimi, but we didn't know he was going to be such a stubborn ass about not admitting it at the time. We thought he was just shooting off his mouth."

"Hmm. Wonder what she came all the way out here to tell him?"

"Probably nothing specific." Bandera grabbed the paddle and began stroking.

"No," Holly said, "women do not drive a couple of hours to say nothing specific."

He shook his head. "She was on her way some-where. This is just a pit stop."

Holly stared at him. He lowered the paddle. "What?"

"You're not really that dense, are you?"

"I suppose I might be. You think she had an ulterior motive?"

Holly laughed. "Bandera, I'll make a bet with you, and this one's safer than all of you betting on whether Mason would stop her wedding."

He perked up. "I like the sound of a friendly wager. What's on the table?"

"I bet you Mimi came out here with something really, really earth-shattering to tell Mason."

"I thought you'd already established that."

"No fair," she said. "You weren't certain she'd had an ulterior motive when she stopped here."

He put the paddle down, and now that they were safely hidden from the shore by trees, he took her hands and pulled her toward him. "Spell it out for me some more. I love to watch your lips when you talk. They're so full. They *enunciate* so well."

She pushed him away when he would have stolen a kiss. "This is a *serious* wager, Bandera."

"Oh, sure, get serious on me now, when we're in the middle of a creek, and there's no one around, and I want you to kiss me to sweeten the wager."

"No sweetening. I haven't even gotten to the wager yet."

"Hey!" Jellyfish called loudly across the water. He rang a dinner triangle noisily.

"Wow," Bandera said. "I think Jelly wants us to come eat."

"I am hungry," Holly said. "I didn't eat breakfast because I was nervous about getting married."

"And right you were to skip that meal," he said happily. He called back to Jellyfish to tell him that they were coming back in. "Quick, wager me."

"All right. The bet is that Mimi drove all the way here because she has something really important to tell Mason. If I'm right, you have to...send me a postcard when you get to Alaska."

He frowned. "Did I say I was going to Alaska?"

"You said you had to stay with Mason. He says he's probably headed to Alaska."

"This was supposed to be a simple visit to hire Hawk and Jelly to do the search!" Bandera was outraged. "How do you know all this?"

"Marielle told me. She wanted to know when I might be by to look at her land. I said I was traveling with you for a bit, and she said she wouldn't look for me for at least a week, since Mason was going to Alaska."

"That snake! I'm not only going to push him in the lake, I'm gonna give him the dunking of his life!"

"Hold on," Holly said, laughing at him. "Can't you give him a chance to tell you?"

"No. Because he's not going to until it's too late, obviously." Bandera was so annoyed he didn't know what to do. "Hey, that means...you should have gone back with Cousin Mike and Marielle. How come you didn't?"

She raised her chin. "There are planes, buses, trains and rental cars from just about anywhere, Bandera Jefferson. I felt like traveling a little longer, but don't get any cockier than you already are. I am happy right now just to be on the road."

He put a finger under her chin. "You may be telling a bit of a story, Holly Henshaw. I think you like me more than you're letting on."

She pulled away from him. "Even if I did, I wouldn't be stupid enough to tell you." Her gaze went to the shore, where they could make out Mimi and Mason talking in the gathering dusk. "They've got a great thing going."

"No, Holly, they have a really confused thing going."

"They're friends, aren't they?"

"Awesome friends. They love each other like brother and sister."

"No, they don't," she said, laughing. "They *want* to love each other that way. But something's keeping them apart."

"Mason's fat head," he said gruffly.

"You're so mean to your brother." She gave him a tiny pop on the arm, which he thought was cute. She was out in a canoe in the middle of a creek, alone with a man she didn't know very well, and she felt comfortable enough to be playful.

"If I win the bet," he said, "you have to tell me what color your underwear is."

"It's colors," she said slyly, "and you're naughty for asking."

"Colors plural?" He sat up.

"Actually, the absence of all light, and something more," she said cryptically.

He thought about her wedding garter and went totally still. "Not black and white polka dots?"

"You haven't won the bet so I'm not telling," she said. "You have absolutely no regard for rules."

"Oh, man." What was the silly wager, anyway? He couldn't remember. Squeezing Holly's fingers between his, he thought about her softness and her petite bones. She'd be soft and petite all over. His breath stopped; his blood hummed. "I forgot the rules," he said helplessly. "Let's wager something about you and me instead."

"All right," she said, pulling her hand away. "What?"

He blinked, still thinking about what color her undies were. What did a bride wear under her wedding dress? What sort of satin or silk and lace had she planned to reveal to her groom as a gift on their wedding night?

Bandera wasn't sure he could handle knowing.

He wasn't sure he could handle *not* knowing.

"Holly," he said softly, "I'll give you a thousand

dollars to start your business if you tell me what's under those shorts you're wearing.

She stared at him, shocked. "Bandera."

He had never been more serious in his life. "I don't have to see it," he said, putting a dare-you glint in his eyes, "but I want excruciating detail. Color, style, size, fit."

"You're insane."

But she liked him being insane, he noticed, because her skin had goose bumps all over it, even along her delicate arms. *One day,* he told himself, *I'm going to kiss all the way from her wrist up to that fragile white underarm, before I make my way—*

He was lost in his fantasy, so he was a bit slow to realize that her hands had moved to her shorts. He heard snaps give, and she slowly pulled something down.

Mesmerized, he felt real pain from the pounding of his heart.

She took his hand and pressed something into the palm.

It was her panties, still warm from her body. His mouth dried out; he got the fastest, hardest erection he'd ever had in his life.

Thong. Black lace waistband. Tiny little crotch of white with black iridescent sequins. Polka dots. Snaps on the sides.

"You win," he said. "Whatever we were betting about, you win."

THEY'D HEADED BACK TO shore in utter silence. Bandera hadn't said another word; he'd just handed her panties back to her quickly, then begun paddling.

Clearly, he could dish it out but not take it.

Holly hopped out of the canoe at the water's edge, helped him pull the boat ashore so that it was once again wedged in its place, then began walking away.

Her breath caught when Bandera swooped her up in his arms. "Bandera!"

"You are a little minx," he said, his voice a growl next to her ear. "I have never, ever had a woman strip for me like you just did. I didn't get to see a thing under those shorts, but somehow, you got me hotter than a pistol."

"Bang, bang," she said, goading him.

"Holly," he said, crushing her against his chest, "you had no business trying to marry some poor sap who couldn't handle you. I've made up my mind for the both of us. The only one who's going to be handling you is *me*. And it's going to have very little to do with business."

BANDERA LET HOLLY scramble down out of his arms and run toward the cabin. He didn't mind. She'd scared him with the panty trick; now he'd scared her with the hot he-man routine.

He relished a good game of push-pull. Hadn't he warned her that he had the stamina for a long chase?

He closed his eyes for a second, wishing he'd kept her panties. There'd been nothing there but air, basically. Airy lace. "Now that would be a name for a hot air balloon," he said to himself.

Holly was seated at the kitchen table when he walked in, along with everyone else. A chair had been left next to her, so he took it, leaning down to whisper, "Best thousand dollars I ever spent," into her ear.

Her blush delighted him. She nearly knocked over her tea, and he grinned.

"Want to make another wager?" he asked, so low that only she could hear him as the assembled company began passing around dishes of food.

"No."

"Oh, come on."

She sniffed and ladled some steaming mashed potatoes onto her plate, next to a beautifully grilled piece of meat and some brussels sprouts.

"I have a thousand dollars," she said brightly.

"I know. You just won it from me."

"Double or nothing," she said, turning to look him straight in the eye.

He grinned. The chase was on.

"Terms?"

She took a deep breath. "I'll bet you that you can't forgo talking about making love or anything to do with sexual contact between two people for the next twenty-four hours. That includes kissing, my lips, and anything else romantic."

He frowned. "You want a moratorium on romance?"

"Yes," she said. "Twenty-four hours of just being my friend, like Mason is Mimi's."

Their voices had risen to conversation level, and they realized everyone else was listening. Holly's blush deepened, and Bandera sat back in his chair, looking at her.

He definitely wanted to catch his little bride-on-the-run. So if she wanted to be friends…he was a pretty friendly guy. "Friends it is," he said. "You have trust issues, but I'm understanding."

She hesitated, a fork in her hand. "I do not."

"It's okay. I've spent an entire day with you, and I know everything about you that I need to. I'll wait for you to know everything about me that you need to."

Mason cleared his throat. "Would you two care to take this outside?"

Mimi's eyes were huge and wide as she stared at them. Jellyfish and Hawk were grinning.

"I thought you were never going to get a girl-friend," Hawk said.

"Something about the road less traveled," Jellyfish chimed in. "Something about poetry being better read alone."

"Yes." Bandera calmly buttered a roll. "But I've

had second thoughts. I can live like you three, or I can try to enjoy the mysteries of life. You," he said to Hawk, "live in the wilderness and seem fairly happy. Jellyfish, you're a man of mystery and means, and probably committed to nothing but whatever hippie ideal jolts you."

Jellyfish grinned. Hawk nodded.

"But I am a Jefferson," Bandera said, "and when I look at Mason, I think there has to be a better way."

His brother laid his fork down. "What the hell does that mean?"

Bandera shrugged. "Whatever you think it means. I'm taking this lady on a walk. Would you like to come, Holly?"

She jumped up from the table. "Excuse me, everyone. I have something to say to Indiana Jones here."

Bandera opened the door for Holly. "Don't bother clearing our plates. We'll be back. The food's awesome, Hawk."

He closed the door.

"You're probably going to have a long wait," she told Bandera once they were alone. "I like my life the way it is. I can't see any reason to change it."

"Essentially, neither can I. You already cut loose all the deadwood. Now you're ready to flower."

"Bandera!"

He laughed, taking her hand and pulling her down

a path toward the creek. "You know this is a ton more fun than a honeymoon with Useless."

She sighed. "You do make me feel better, but then I feel guilty because I know I should probably slap you for your cockiness."

"Why slap me when you really want to kiss me?" He pulled her into his arms. "Guess I just lost that bet."

"You make me crazy," she said. "I don't know what to think about you. You're sort of weird, but in an okay way, and I really don't know what my parents would think about you."

"Ah, they would think a wolf had grabbed their lamb, which I intend to do." He kissed her, his hands moving along her back, guiding her toward him.

"Yes, but—" She broke away. "I would rather make my own way. Like Mimi."

"Oh, no," he said. "You don't want to hold Mimi up as a role model. I already told you that. Trust me, she makes Mason as nervous as a cat around dogs."

"But she came to him," Holly said. "And that's what I'm trying to tell you. I don't want to be overwhelmed, romanced, swept away or otherwise caught. This time, I want to do the choosing. I want to fall slowly. You're not a fall slowly kind of guy." She touched his face softly. "I'm sorry. I don't mean to hurt your feelings. But with you, I know it's all or nothing."

"That's true," Bandera said.

"I want to be nothing for a while," she said. "In general. I need time to think."

He swallowed, his heart shriveling. She was totally serious about this, and he sensed that if he pushed her, he'd lose her forever. "I'm sorry if I've come on too strong. It's sort of my nature, as you've noticed."

This time, she took his hand and moved in next to him. "I've noticed that with your family and friends, it's all pretty much a walk on the wild side. I really admire that. I do." She took a deep breath. "But think about it. I'm a virgin, as you know from overhearing my phone conversation. One who lives very close to her parents, and who does nothing more exciting than plan weddings for a living."

"Sounds pretty explosive to me."

Smiling, she shook her head. "No. I had my life all planned out." She frowned. "But today was a slight bump I wasn't anticipating."

"I like the way you handled it."

She looked up at him. "At first I thought you were trying to make me feel better by being so attentive. But now I think you might just be a rogue, enjoying a flirtation."

"Rogue. I like the sound of that. Bandera the rogue."

She tapped his chest. "Pay attention here. I'm trying my best to be honest."

"So far I'm coming off pretty heroic. Continue."

She took a deep breath. "Okay. But then I met Mimi—"

"Blast Mimi. Something about her soured my game plan."

Holly laughed. "No. But you can see how much she and Mason like each other."

"You can?" Bandera put his arms around Holly as sneakily as he could. Maybe while she was busy philosophizing, she wouldn't notice him enjoying how great she felt. Never had he encountered such soft skin, such smoothness. Almost like the meringue his mother used to put on the tops of pies at Christmas.

"You are definitely not paying attention," she told him. "And I believe you're copping a feel."

He let go of her bra strap. "Sorry."

She smiled. "No, you're not." Stepping away from him, she looked up, searching his eyes. "I hope you understand."

He was still thinking about the tiny bra strap at her back. When he was young, he'd gained the very elementary skill of undoing a bra with one hand. It was no harder than throwing a lasso just right, or hanging on to a saddle horn. The challenge was in the timing.

His timing was clearly off. "I think so. You want to be friends."

"Well, friends who care about each other."

He sighed. "All right. I can handle rejection with the best of them. I have been thrown before and lived."

"Come on," she said. "Let's go eat that wonderful supper."

"And then what?"

"I've vacationed enough," she said. "I'd like to go home and do some planning."

"More planning," he grumbled good-naturedly. "To think I almost had you in action mode."

"If I'm going to start a new business, it will take lots of planning."

"Hey, I'm still in on that."

"Good. Business partners will be a lot more fun than being…whatever it was you had in mind."

He grinned. No, business partnerships weren't more fun than other kinds of…partnerships.

But she didn't know that.

For now, he sensed it was best to let her run her rope for a while—before he ever so gently pulled her back in.

She smiled at him, and he tweaked her nose gently.

He was okay with "just friends." Time was on his side.

Eventually she would come to him.

Chapter Eight

Holly walked back inside with Bandera, feeling good and yet somehow bad about the conversation they'd just had. The truth was, she had been flattered by his attention. But he was so handsome, so sure of himself that he was scaring her a bit.

She needed some time to figure things out. After all, she'd just made a colossal mistake.

Bandera was so much temptation she feared she might use him to rebound, based on her crushed dreams. It would be too easy to fall into this man's very willing arms.

But it wasn't nice to lead someone on, and she didn't know if she'd ever be able to find joy in another relationship. Romance seemed to be wired with booby traps.

For now, though, she'd just enjoy Bandera's company and a meal with his friends.

"Mason," Mimi said a little while later as she pushed away her plate, "I think I'll head on back."

He seemed surprised. "What's the rush?"

"You have somewhere to go. I have a baby waiting at home."

"Well, okay, if you want." He stood. "But we were planning on bunking here for the night, and then head out at first light. Jelly and Hawk and I want to talk over some plans. So don't rush off."

Mimi hesitated. Holly could practically feel the other woman's indecision. Half of her wanted to stay, half of her knew she should go.

Holly completely understood. Bandera made her feel like that.

"Hey, Mimi," Mason said, "stay awhile longer."

Bandera blinked. Hawk and Jellyfish raised their heads. Holly tried to look busy rearranging her napkin. How could Mimi resist the plea in that voice? she wondered.

Mimi blushed. "If Holly's staying, I suppose I could."

Holly glanced up, startled. Now that was a new angle! "I am staying tonight, but if you're changing your plans and leaving in the morning, could you give me a ride?"

"That would be great." Mimi smiled. "It would be wonderful to have a woman to visit with on the drive. I'd really enjoy getting to know you."

"Great," Bandera said. "Thelma and Louise all over again."

Mason started to say something, his mouth opening and closing, then he finally just shut it.

"Sounds like everything is worked out," Hawk said, getting to his feet. "In the morning, we four men will ride out to Alaska. You two ladies will find spiritual comfort in each other as you return home."

The table fell silent at that pronouncement.

Holly wondered why she felt so awkward. She had to leave sooner or later. Bandera was just a momentary fling. His attention, his sense of adventure—none of that was right for her in the long term. As a student of life she was cautious.

Business partners, maybe. Anything more, no.

"I'll be ready when you are, Mimi," Holly said brightly, taking her dishes into the kitchen, already knowing she would miss Bandera like crazy.

HAWK AND JELLY MADE a campfire outside, studying maps for two hours after dinner. Holly was holed up in a guest room. Mason listened to the men plan their trip, sometimes answering questions, and Mimi sat beside him, their arms not touching.

Bandera rubbed dirt off his boot toe as he sat at the campfire. Okay, so it was early June, and they could have done this planning stuff inside, but Jelly's house was a tax address, not really a place of comfort. His home was the outdoors. In fact, he often slept in a sleeping bag on the porch or in the woods along the water. Sometimes he retired to the pier so he could hear the fish jump and the birds and insects move in the trees at night.

Bandera got up and tossed out his original goal of following Mason—even to Alaska. He knocked on Holly's door.

When she opened it, his gut slid over, despite his best attempt not to stare at her in her long white gown with streaming satin ribbons. He'd like to say it wasn't sexy, but he couldn't. The top was held up with thin straps, and the sides were cut out. It was basically see-through, and the lamp on the table backlit her.

Damn, he thought, *there is no way we can be just friends.* "Ah," he said, backing away from the door, "I'm sorry. I thought maybe you were watching TV. I didn't realize you were in bed."

She looked at him, her face sweet and innocent. "Was there something you wanted?"

"Yes. I mean, no!" He gathered his wits, taking a deep breath. "That's a beautiful, uh, nightgown." The second he told her, he wished he hadn't. Even as a schoolboy he hadn't been this uncertain; he'd had the one-handed bra strap removal down cold. Why did this woman make him feel as though his every breath felt better, deeper, more alive, when he was with her?

"Thank you. It's my wedding nightgown." She smiled at him. "No point in it going to waste, I decided. This is the closest to a real wedding night that I'll get."

He was trembling, or at least his hands were. His blood felt funny; his mind seemed confused. All he could register was that this woman should be his, and yet she was innocently unaware of that fact.

"I was going to see if you wanted to take a walk," he said, trying bravely not to look below her waist and finally giving up. If he ever got married, he was going to fill his home with lamps—cheery, homey little lamps that sent a glow right through any fabric on a woman's body. His wife was going to wear nothing but sheer fabric, when she wore anything at all. "I'm sorry I disturbed you."

He turned to walk away, trying to keep his lust from blowing out his brain function. Everything in his body screamed that he should go into that room and make love to that woman. He could teach her that some things were better when they weren't planned. Without her groom, tonight was going to be lonely, and he wanted to show her that every night with *him* could seem like a real wedding night.

But she'd asked him to be friends. She needed time.

Trust was even more important than sex, and he had to let her know that he understood.

Even if it killed him.

IN THE MORNING, Bandera found that Holly had already left with Mimi. Mason stood by the remains of the campfire from the night before. Jelly and Hawk were nowhere to be seen, but they'd left a note that said they'd made a run for some supplies.

"I wonder what supplies one can find at six o'clock in the morning," Bandera said, "and at what store. I didn't see anything with a sign on it between here and Hawk's."

Mason grunted.

"So did Mimi say goodbye to you?"

"No. I came out here this morning to find her truck gone."

"The least Holly could have done was say goodbye," Bandera said. He'd never had a woman disappear on him like that before.

"She owed you nothing," Mason said. "The way you had your paws all over her, she was probably glad you slept in."

"I did not…" He stopped, annoyed. So he had kissed her as often as he'd dared. He'd also respected her need to be alone, though it had been difficult. "I knew she wouldn't hang around," he said miserably. "She was too good to be true."

"Hell, Mimi didn't hang around, either, and she's always been too good to be true."

Bandera stared at his brother, shocked. "How

come you don't act like you think she's too good to
be true when she's around?"

"Because." Mason sounded surprised. "There are
thoughts in that brain no man will ever understand,
nor should he attempt to."

"Mason, man, Mimi *loves* you." Bandera stared at
his brother.

Mason waved his hands in protest. "You don't understand. Mimi loves everyone. It's not a long-term
thing. I ought to know that better than anyone," he
said with a sigh.

"What in the hell does that mean?"

"It means," Mason said slowly, "that Miss Mimi
and I have a secret no one knows. Not a single soul
on the planet."

Bandera blinked. "I'm all ears."

"And nosy, too," Mason growled. "Let's just say
that I know all too well how Holly feels."

Bandera suddenly had the wildest notion that
Mason had more of a grip on things than any of the
brothers ever suspected; he'd just been keeping his
feelings to himself all this time. *And we thought he
was an unfeeling ass.*

"I know what it feels like to have the person you
love marry someone else," Mason said gruffly.

Bandera frowned. "Earth to Mason. You've never
told any woman you love her."

"I'm not laying claim to it, so don't ask me to,"

his brother said. "But let's just say Mimi and I had one night where we nearly talked it all out."

A cold wind, contrary to the June morning heat, swept through Bandera. "Wait," he said, grabbing his brother's sleeve as Mason turned away, "you're not saying you and Mimi—"

Mason jerked his sleeve out of Bandera's grasp. "I'm not saying any damn thing, except this—you need to take some time to figure out what you really want with that Holly girl. If you decide she's the one, then don't let her out of your sight."

Mason walked away. Bandera stared after his brother, his jaw slack with wonder. "Mason has feelings," he said to himself. "He's not an unemotional blockhead."

He was mildly jealous that Mason and Holly had found they had so much in common. They understood each other as friends.

Bandera, however, couldn't see past Holly's polka-dotted thong and her sheer gown. Even now, when he thought of her, he got a rise in his Levi's that wouldn't quit. Yes, he desired her; he knew because of the lust that hammered at his body.

But did the feeling resonate from his heart? Was it deep and real, or did he just want Holly because no one else had had her? Did he want her because she was beautiful?

If he wasn't careful, he would end up like Mason,

which would be a fate worse than listening to his brother Crockett ramble on about art.

Holly had left him without saying goodbye, a fact that rankled and ate at Bandera's pride. Why should he go tearing after a woman who didn't want him?

Because, he thought. *Because Mason said so.*

But if anybody knows how to mess something up, it's Mason.

Because if not for Mason, Bandera wouldn't be *here* with three men about to head out on a wild-goose chase—instead of in a truck with two beautiful women.

One of whom had really caught his eye.

"SO THE SCOOP ON THE Jefferson men," Mimi said to Holly as they rode down the interstate, "is that they're different from any other men you may meet."

Holly took that in, watching the countryside pass by. One thing she could say for certain was that Mimi drove much more slowly than Bandera. It was nice and peaceful to see the pretty green landscape as the trees exchanged their spring buds for June finery. "I did notice something different," she finally said. "In a good way."

"They're wonderful. All the Jefferson men are. Their only hang-up is that they have a terrible fear of commitment, most of the time. But in the past couple of years, several of them have *run* to the altar with the ladies they love. Of course, they met really nice women." Mimi smiled. "It's almost as if they know exactly what they want when they see it, and they go after it with everything they've got."

"Do I sense some history between you and Mason?" Holly asked gently. She didn't want to pry, but Mimi seemed to want to talk.

"There's history," she confirmed softly.

"Oh." Holly looked at her newfound friend. Mimi seemed so gentle, so kind. Mason seemed like a cool dude. But Holly was seeing both of them from the outside looking in. There must be a reason they weren't together…Holly's heart ached for Mimi. She loved Mason; it was apparent, even to a stranger.

"I'm sorry," Holly said. "Guys are kind of weird sometimes, as I just found out myself."

Mimi laughed good-naturedly. "Mason's more than weird sometimes. Let's not sugarcoat it."

Relieved, Holly smiled, too. "Okay. We won't."

"And while we're vowing not to get out the artificial sweetener, let's not sugarcoat Bandera, either. Be warned that if you've got your eye on him, you'll have to do some pretty fancy roping."

"Oh, it's not like that," Holly said hurriedly.

"Uh-huh."

"We're going into business together. In fact, Bandera has already put up a thousand dollars on good faith." She politely neglected to mention the money had satisfied his curiosity about her panties. "Polka dots are good luck," she said softly. "I'm going to design a banner for my honeymoon retreat, of a balloon made with white lace and black polka dots."

"Oh, good," Mimi said, "Bandera loves polka dots. He's just dotty for them." She giggled, pleased with herself.

Holly frowned. "It's unusual, isn't it?"

"There is nothing normal about those men, Holly, from the way they were raised to the way they live their lives now. I would offer to help you get through your reluctance phase so you could move into your acceptance phase, but unfortunately, I'm just now moving into my own acceptance phase."

Holly swallowed. "I should probably skip the whole thing. I'm not feeling very strong these days."

Mimi turned to look at her briefly. "Well, tell me something. Have you ever met a man like Bandera?"

Holly could honestly say she had not. "No."

"Are you sure you want to skip it?"

Chapter Nine

"What worries me," Holly said to Mimi as they drove down the tree-lined highway, "is how much I like Bandera. I've never been so incredibly attracted to someone. The second I met him, I wanted to change everything about myself."

"Really?" Mimi asked. "I think Bandera likes you just the way you are."

"That's the problem. He doesn't know who I am. I wanted to be sexy around him. Free-spirited. And that's just not me at all." She sighed. "I even threw my garter through the truck window at him."

Mimi laughed. "Trust me, he loved that."

"And I…gave him my panties on a bet," she whispered. "And the worst part," she added, looking at Mimi, who was trying hard not to giggle, "is that I didn't do it for the money. I gave him my thong just to be a little…"

"Wild." Mimi laughed. "Trust me, Bandera was

very happy that you did. Women always leave lacy calling cards for the Jefferson men. Helga—their housekeeper—is forever muttering about getting some unmentionable in the mail or left at the front door. One enterprising young lady left her white satin nightgown hooked to the stall of one of their horses. That night, the nightgown spooked the horse. Luckily, we were nearby when it went nuts in its stall."

"What became of the girl?"

"Oh, Mason got the gown and the phone number she'd left inside it. It was one of the younger brothers' school friends. Mason called her parents."

"Which brother was the gown intended for?"

"Crockett." Mimi grinned. "He didn't dare ask that girl out after Mason had his fit. Mason said the girl was dumb as a rock and careless to boot, and Crockett knew better than to disagree. It was a pretty nightie, though." She sighed. "They gave it to the church rummage sale, with a lot of other stuff, and I heard Widow—hey, what's that?"

Holly turned to see what Mimi was looking at in her rearview mirror. "It's Bandera!"

"Your voice is so excited when you say his name," Mimi said with a grin.

"I'm just surprised." Holly put her head out the window, waving at him.

"Do you want me to pull over?" Mimi asked. "We

can say we thought he was going back home and wanted to caravan."

Holly pulled her head back inside, straightening her hair with a careless hand. "Isn't he?"

"Unless I miss my guess, he's come after you," Mimi said. "So if you've decided to be brave, now's the time to do it. If you're still feeling anguished—and that's understandable—we'll just keep going, without him."

Holly folded her hands tightly in her lap. Almost every instinct told her to stay with Mimi. Here she was safe. Bandera made her feel things she wasn't ready to feel. Though she now knew she hadn't loved her ex-fiancé, the whole matter had hurt.

"Just keep going," she said. "It's better for both of us."

Mimi looked at her. "Are you sure?"

Holly nodded.

"Wow, this may be a record. The first time a woman has determined she's definitely not giving in to a Jefferson male."

"You didn't give in," Holly said. "Bandera said you and Mason never get your stuff figured out."

"Bandera should mind his own business. Actually, Mason… I love Mason."

"I know," Holly said. "But you still didn't give in and start chasing him."

"Actually, I do chase him every once in a while," Mimi said with a sigh. "And sometimes I think he's chasing me. Then we both get nervous and back off. I don't really know. I've got to get it figured out soon." She laughed. "Bandera's flashing his lights at us. He wants me to pull over."

"This is precisely what I mean," Holly said nervously. "Bandera said he had a lot of stamina for chasing me, or something like that."

"Oh. He said that?" Mimi looked pensive. "You know, sometimes I get tired of cocky Jefferson attitude. Even though I find it attractive and sexy as hell, every once in a while, I think *What the hell, buddy?*"

Holly smiled. "I can understand that."

"So, if you're sure you don't want to swap seats and ride with him—"

"I'm fine for now," she said hurriedly. "Thanks."

"Then you and I are going to ignore him and his flashing lights." Mimi jumped when her cell phone rang, quickly checking the screen. "Ah. It's probably for you," she said. "Bandera."

Holly took the phone. "Hello?"

"Hey. Come ride with me," he said. "You and I need to plan our business."

"I'm happy with Mimi," Holly said stubbornly.

"Yeah, but she listens to bad music on the radio. And I'm much more interesting."

"We're having girl chat," Holly said.

"Is that why my ears are burning?" he asked. "Talking about me, are you?"

"We were talking about Mason, actually," she said.

"Oh. Mason always gets to be the object of affection," he complained. "And conversation. Unless one of us does something really crazy."

Holly tried not to let him lure her. "Don't do anything crazy," she said. "We're enjoying talking about Mason."

He sighed. "I'm coming on too strong for you, aren't I?"

"Yeah." She nodded to emphasize her point, even though he couldn't see. "You're too strong, and I'm too weak right now."

"I hate this," Bandera said softly.

"I just don't want to be dishonest."

"All right," he murmured. "I understand."

"Do you?" She wanted him to.

"Yeah. So I'll just follow you back to Malfunction Junction, and you just pretend I'm not here."

"Malfunction what?"

"Junction. Our ranch."

Holly blinked. "Your ranch is named Malfunction Junction?"

"Well, that's what folks in town call it, and it stuck. We decided we like it. Sometimes, anyway."

"Now that would be interesting on wedding invitations," she said thoughtfully. "Formal wedding reception at Malfunction Junction—"

"See?" he said happily. "Let's do it."

He nearly made her smile with his spontaneity. "Nobody leaves one man and accepts another in two days. Particularly not a proposal over a cell phone from a man she doesn't know that well."

"Getting to know me is the fun part," Bandera said. "Help me not end up like Mason. Old and curmudgeonly."

She laughed. "Mason's not old and curmudgeonly."

"He can be a bit ornery," Mimi said, putting her two cents in.

"You kissed me like you knew me," Bandera reminded Holly, "and I enjoyed it."

Holly blushed and was glad he couldn't see. "That was the wild in me surfacing. I've calmed down now."

"Mimi's a bad influence," he griped. "Tell her no more calming. I like you wild. I'm trying to liberate you. In ways you can't even imagine. You can be my really wild Barbie doll."

Her eyes went wide. "Is that how you see me? As a Barbie doll?"

Mimi snorted.

"Much more individual, but cute and leggy, yeah," he said. "Not so much boobs. Definitely more flexible—"

"Bandera, you are living in an era of chauvinism long past."

"And you find it appealing," he said. "Tell Mimi to stop the truck so you can slap me."

"No." He was so going to seduce her if she wasn't careful. Her willpower was starting to slip. "Bad boy wants good girl isn't going to work."

"Huh. It always works."

"Not this time."

He sighed. "All right. Here's a new role—good girl wants good man. And you should."

"Bandera!"

"Dang it," Mimi said. "My truck's overheating."

"Oh, no!" Holly looked at the gauge. "Are you sure?"

"I am so sure, hot lady," Bandera said. "I am not the kind of man who changes his mind."

"That's not what I meant," Holly said hastily. "Mimi's truck is overheating."

"Are you sure?" he asked.

"That's what I just said!"

"Sorry," he replied. "I was trying to elaborate my position."

"And you have. Succinctly. What should we do?"

"About me and you? Or the truck?"

"There is no me and you, because I am not going to be a woman on the rebound. 'Rebound bride' has a terrible ring to it."

"Hmm. You have a point. Although I would never call you that. It's my personal opinion that the wedding you ran from was only a dress rehearsal for the real, genuine big day in your life.

Tell Mimi to pull over, well off the road, on the shoulder."

Holly hung up and handed the phone back to Mimi. "Bandera says to pull over."

"It's amazing how the Jefferson men always end up with everything going their way," Mimi complained. "My poor old truck."

Carefully, she slowed down and pulled off the road to park. "At least Nanette wasn't in the car when this happened. She doesn't have much interest in being stranded, or sitting still."

Holly got out of the truck. Bandera had already pulled up behind them. Climbing out, he walked past Holly and gestured for Mimi to pop the hood.

Holly stood beside him, peering at whatever he was looking at. "Does it need water?"

"I don't know. But steam is not a good sign."

Puffs of air were escaping from under the radiator cap. Holly frowned. "I don't think you should touch it."

"I won't." He grinned, rubbing her back. "Guess what? You get to ride with me."

She tried not to melt. She refused to look into his eyes. She pulled away. "I've been thinking," she said.

"You mean you've been talking to Mimi," he said. "Mimi's like my sister, and you know how little sisters always talk about their brothers. They're not the most reliable, objective source of information."

Holly grabbed her purse from inside Mimi's truck. "Mimi, can I help you carry anything?"

"No, thank you. I've got everything."

The three of them scooted into the truck, with Mimi making certain she got to the back seat first. That left Holly to sit up front with Bandera, because if she got in the back it would be too obvious a move.

"All I ask is that you don't touch my radio," Bandera said in a lordly tone. "We'll get along just fine."

"This is Mason's truck," Mimi reminded him from the back seat. "Technically, she can touch—"

"This is what I'm talking about, the sisterly thing," Bandera interrupted. "You see she gives me little to no respect." He turned around to look at Mimi. "Quiet as a mouse, now."

Mimi snorted. "Pipe down, brother."

"There." Bandera made certain Holly was buckled in securely, then drove off. "Everything's back to normal."

"It's not normal. My truck's overheated," Mimi wailed.

"I called Shoeshine Johnson. He'll head this way to look at it. Unless you want me to call Triple A or something."

"No." Mimi sighed. "Shoeshine's fine. Nobody knows vehicles like him."

"Shoeshine?" Holly said. "Is that his given name?"

"Yeah, given to him by everybody in town." Bandera patted her knee. "Do you have a nickname?"

"No!"

He laughed. Mimi did, too. So Holly settled back into the seat, relaxing, because it was kind laughter. Playful. Something she hadn't had...in nearly a year, she realized. She'd been so busy planning, planning for nothing, with no time for laughter or fun.

She'd gotten too tied up in details that weren't important, and she'd forgotten about the good things. These people made her happy. She liked them all: Mimi, Bandera, Mason, Jellyfish, Hawk...and she'd only met a few members of the family.

Suddenly, she felt sad. She would probably never meet the rest of the brothers. Or Shoeshine and Helga. All the people Bandera spoke of so easily... They seemed like one big happy family, getting on each other's nerves but loving each other, too.

"So how is my little niece?" Bandera asked. "I need to come get her for her next pony ride."

"She'll like that."

Holly hadn't thought of Bandera as being the "uncle" type, but the note of caring in his voice was unmistakable.

"She's a special little thing," Bandera told Holly. "Makes a man want to write poetry when she pats your face with those little fingers and says, 'Pony, Uncle Bandera.'"

Holly smiled at him. "So you do have a gentle side."

He shook his head. "No. Just for that little one. And Calhoun and Olivia's kids. Now those two are a piece of work. They can keep you hopping all day if you let them." A grin crossed his face. "Minnie and Kenny make you wish you had kids of your own."

Mimi leaned forward, her arms crossed on the seat as she looked at Bandera. "I don't remember you ever saying that before. You're beginning to sound like a proud father."

"Uncle!" he corrected. "I like the uncle role. I can't really see myself as a father."

The two women nodded.

"On the other hand," he said crossly, "I can't really see myself not being a father."

Holly laughed. "You don't know what you want."

He stared at her. "Yes, I do."

She turned quickly to look out the window, startled.

Mimi thumped him lightly on the shoulder. "Rein it in a bit, wild man. Put your club away."

He sighed. "So, Mimi, how's your dad?"

Bandera's fingers touched Holly's side, giving her a little pinch. For some reason, it felt like sort of an apology. An I-didn't-mean-to-scare-you type of thing. Holly looked at him, wondering why he was so persistent, and why she was beginning to appreciate his attention so much.

"Well, I have to admit," Mimi said, "the move to

town agrees with him. He's got my little girl, which surely started him on the road to recovery—a miracle, the doctors said. He's got Barley, who visits frequently, and widows dropping by with pies."

"Mmm," Holly said. "That would make me happy. Especially in the fall. No, even in the summer. Apple pie."

"You're making me hungry!" Bandera said. "Hawk and Jellyfish made up a breakfast of twigs and branches this morning, survival stuff. I'm not too sorry to be missing the trip to Alaska."

"What made you change your mind, Bandera?" Mimi asked in a sisterly, mocking jest.

Holly's eyes widened. Bandera's fingers tweaked her forearm lightly, where Mimi couldn't see.

"I knew Thelma and Louise would probably need my assistance," he explained. "It seemed like a bad idea, two girls going off in a truck by themselves."

"Whatever," Mimi said, laughing.

"We would have been just fine," Holly declared, joining in.

"Okay," Bandera said. "Just suppose I buy that lie for now. Be good girls and say that the trip home is much better with a big, strong guy like me."

Holly and Mimi laughed.

He sighed, pretending to be hurt. "Or not. So, Mimi, what was the errand that brought you all the way out by Hawk's and Jelly's, anyway?"

In that second, Holly felt tension return to the truck.

Mimi put her face down on her forearms. "Well, I've got this big problem."

Bandera turned serious, going into protective brother mode. Holly watched his expression go from poking fun to true concern—and the change amazed her.

"Anything I can do?"

Mimi shook her head. "Not really."

"This has to do with Mason, right? Or were you coming to seek his counsel?"

Mimi's gaze dropped. "I needed to talk to him."

"Mimi," Bandera said. "Everything's fine with the sheriff, right? And our little girl?"

Holly looked at Mimi, seeing distress in her blue eyes. "Bandera," Holly said, "I should probably switch seats with Mimi. I could take a nap in the back while you two discuss this."

"No, it's fine," Mimi said quickly. "I've got myself in a big mess, and I could probably use an objective opinion from someone who is not Mason's brother."

"I may be his brother," Bandera said, "but I'm also yours. You know that, Mimi."

"I do," she said softly. "I've just been running and running. Too afraid to slow down. It started when Dad got sick. I was so frightened. I wanted him to be happy. The doctors said he was probably going to die—"

"I personally thought he was at the end of his days

on earth," Bandera said. "It was crazy how quick he got worse."

"Liver infection," Mimi told Holly. "And though my dad is strong, and tough, and a fighter, there was awhile there where…"

Holly looked away as she realized Mimi was tearing up. She dug around in her bag, producing the tissues she'd put in there to dry her own tears over her nonwedding. Turned out she hadn't needed the travel pack, she thought gratefully, handing them over the seat to Mimi with a sidelong glance at Bandera.

Every woman who had a wedding go awry should have a man like Bandera to make her feel like a queen again.

"So," Mimi said, "I think I went wild, worrying about Dad. I remembered what a mischief maker I'd been as a girl—"

"An understatement," Bandera agreed. "We all raised hell for the sheriff, but you were definitely the ringleader."

Holly smiled. "Sort of like those stories about the preacher's kids."

"It's true," Mimi admitted. "I didn't have a mother, really, to keep me in check. Dad was gone a lot. I found things to do that kept me—"

"Mimi," Bandera interrupted. "You can't blame yourself without blaming us, too. We were right there with you."

"You seem so upright," Holly said. "I'm amazed at this story."

He patted her leg. "You have no idea how much disaster twelve boys and one ringleading girl can wreak upon a small town when left to their own devices. Although I will say," he mused, "that Mason was kind of a pain in the ass. Always trying to be moral, dragging our butts to church every Sunday. Man, he's always been a pill."

Mimi laughed, wiping her eyes. "I shook him loose every once in a while."

Bandera gazed at her in the rearview mirror. "Thank God for you, Mimi, or we would have all gone mad. At least you could lead him astray occasionally. And you know what? Sometimes the best, most righteous men love a little bit of bad girl."

Mimi laughed.

"You weren't really bad, though. It was all just Mimi-fun. And your daddy loved you when you made messes, Mimi. He was proud. You were like a son, only better, because you were so pretty."

"He had all of y'all to be his sons," Mimi said. "Bandera, I married Brian to give my father a chance to see me happily married."

Bandera's fingers tightened on Holly's forearm. Her heart beat faster as she realized he was reaching out to her for comfort.

"I know," he said simply. "We all knew that. Except for Mason, and I think he just never thought about it. Stubborn donkey."

"You knew?" Mimi asked, surprised.

Bandera nodded. "Yeah. It was so obvious. The sheriff took sick, and you took over. We understood you wanted your daddy to see you with a stable home life, Mimi. Heck, people get married for a thousand different reasons. We liked Brian, even if he was a bit on the fancy side."

Mimi tried to laugh, but it ended a sobbing hiccup. "He's a nice man."

Bandera turned to look at Holly. "Brian still does legal work for the family when we need him. He is a pretty cool guy, except for being fancy, as I say. Never even ridden a horse in his life, I don't think, has he, Mimi?"

She didn't answer. Holly turned to look at her. "Mimi? Are you all right? There are some drinks in a cooler in the back, if you need something—"

"Brian and I were never really married, if you know what I mean," she stated quietly.

Holly turned to look at Bandera, wondering what was actually being said.

But Bandera knew the second she said it. His jaw dropped, and his neck went tight with corded tension as his eyes grew big in his face.

"Oh, heck, Mimi," he said, "trust you to drop the bombshell of all time."

Chapter Ten

Bandera couldn't believe his ears—but his soul knew it was true. Nanette had her mother's beauty, her wit, her passion for fun—and every ounce of Mason's stubbornness. Mimi's spoiled assurance that life was full of cherries to be picked; Mason's confident knowledge that his choices were the right ones.

"Oh, boy," Bandera said, "I've got myself my own little niece. Not that she was any less of a niece before, but she's flesh and blood.... Now I'm going to override Mason's objections and buy her her own pony. She needs to learn show riding. Maybe barrel racing."

Mimi smiled and looked at Holly. "Sorry. Didn't mean to catch you up in this."

"Actually, I'm thrilled to be part of it," she exclaimed, making a fierce pride burst inside Bandera. "I feel as though I witnessed a birth."

"It is a birth," Bandera agreed, "'cause Mason's

gonna act like this child sprang from his forehead, as Zeus did with one of his relations."

Mimi giggled with relief and blew her nose. "Bandera, you can't believe how many times I've wanted to tell Mason. But always in my heart I knew he wasn't ready to be a father. He wasn't ready to hear it. Not from me, anyway."

Bandera sighed. It was, unfortunately, true. Mason had resisted Mimi for so long that they'd all begun to accept it. "You see? You'd fit right in with us," Bandera told Holly. "We tend to go at everything backward."

"Not true," Mimi said. "We just see things from a different angle."

Holly smiled. "I've enjoyed meeting your extended family. I might not have made it through my unfortunate incident if you hadn't found me," she said to Bandera.

"Gratitude is good, isn't it?" he said with a wink.

"Probably not good enough," Holly responded spritely.

"Oh, well," Mimi said from the back seat. "I feel as though you're my sister, Holly. Both of us with weddings that didn't go off as we'd planned."

"Yours was a pretty wedding, though, Mimi," Bandera said. "You should have seen her, Holly. Your wedding planner heart would have been amazed."

Holly smiled at Mimi. "I bet you were a beautiful bride."

"So did Brian know you were, um, expecting when he married you?" Bandera asked.

"Oh. Yes." Mimi tore some tissue and sat back in the seat. "We had an arrangement. He was Dad's lawyer, you know, so he knew how to draw things up. Plus he was willing to keep it strictly friendly between us, because all I wanted at that point was a name for my baby, and my father to die happy, thinking I had a family of my own." She sighed. "Holly, I know this all must sound cold-blooded to you, but truthfully, when I found out my father was dying, I just wasn't myself."

"So…I mean, I know this question may be indelicate, but…" Bandera hesitated. "It's just that I don't recall you and Mason having any type of…you know. Relationship."

"We didn't. We haven't. One night does not a relationship make," Mimi said.

"Ohh," Bandera said. That was true. He'd had one night in Holly's presence, and they didn't have a damn thing to go on, except for the overwhelming feeling that he should be making love to her.

"I was really, really upset one night when Dad was in the hospital," Mimi said, "and Mason—"

"That's good. That's all I need," Bandera interrupted, feeling the back of his neck go red. "I wonder if I should kick some sense into my big brother."

"Why?" Holly asked. "He didn't know. He

doesn't even suspect. It's no fun to be the unsuspecting party, I can tell you."

"So what do you suggest?" Bandera asked. "As Mimi says, she's in a bit of a mess. Which, if I may say, you've handled admirably. I wish I'd been more helpful, but truthfully, for the longest time none of us could figure out what the deal was between you and Brian. We knew something wasn't all it should be, but Mason was always acting like he had a sore tooth, and then Last had his problems with Valentine, and frankly, we just tried to stay out of your business."

"I know. It was better that way, I think. And it's all worked out for the best," Mimi said. "I didn't want Mason to marry me because of a baby. I wanted him to…well, to love me. To want me to be his wife. So I can't say I regret anything I've done. It's just that lately I've realized my daughter deserves to know who her father is."

Mimi took a deep breath. "To her, all the male influences in her life have come from my dad, Calhoun's father-in-law Barley, and the Jefferson brothers. Mostly Mason."

"Yeah, and you probably hate to mess up a good thing. No telling how Mason might react. It could be good, but…" Bandera frowned. "It could also be very bad. So?" he said with a glance at Holly. "Miss Wedding Planner? Do you think the status quo should stay the way it is?"

"I just plan weddings," Holly said, "I don't do relationships. But judging from what little I saw of Mason, I don't think finding out he's a father is going to, um—"

Bandera looked at her. "Make him want to marry Mimi?"

"Well, he'd offer, but it wouldn't be what Mimi wants."

"I know," Mimi stated. "I've always known that."

"And yet," Bandera said, "the Jefferson in me says his daughter has a right to our name. I'll marry you, Mimi."

Mimi laughed. "Thank you, Bandera. I love you, too."

Bandera took Holly's hand in his. "And you're going to be my concubine."

Both women slapped him on the shoulder at the same time.

"Ow!" He chuckled, enjoying the attention. "Ah, life is good. I'm a real uncle, not that I wasn't before, but—"

"Bandera, we know what you mean," Mimi said. "Thank you for trying to be sensitive."

He couldn't wipe the smile off his face. "I think she has my nose, by the way. The Jefferson stubborn nose."

"I think…" Holly said. "Mason *does* have a deep love of family."

Bandera and Mimi stared at her.

"That's true," he finally admitted. "It will hurt his feelings that he didn't know about Nanette. Here's a man who's out desperately searching for the past, when the future is right under his nose."

They sat silently after that. Bandera wanted to reach for Holly's hand again, but she'd pulled away a few moments ago, and if there was one thing he'd learned, it was that determined people didn't like to be pushed.

There had to be that something more between a man and a woman for it to be right—and Bandera was going to find out what was needed between him and Holly to get a yes out of her.

"There's your balloon festival," he told Holly as they passed it. "And your newest business."

"Really?" Mimi asked. "This is what you were talking about?"

A balloon floated serenely above them in the sky. They could see it through the front window of the truck. The people in the basket looked very small, almost invisible.

A chase vehicle passed by, following the balloon, with the balloon's colors emblazoned on the SUV door.

"A hot air balloon honeymoon retreat," Holly said, and Bandera heard the dreamy note in her voice. "Something different, something that no one else has to offer."

He thought Holly had plenty to offer that no one else had. "We're going to be partners," Bandera said.

"I heard," Mimi stated. "Something about a thousand dollars up front."

Bandera glanced at Holly, who blushed.

"Planning fee," Mimi said, her voice teasing.

"That's what it was," Bandera agreed, going along with the ribbing because he knew Mimi meant it in fun. "Have to pay the planner."

But the second he said it, he knew Holly wasn't planning him into the picture at all. Her head was turned so she could look out the side window. When she swung back around to look at him, there was no smile on her face.

She seemed just as preoccupied as Mason had been when he'd left for the north.

Bandera had to do something. He had to win her over. "Shall we stop?" he asked. "Fish around for info on your investment dreams?"

"I'd love that," Holly agreed instantly, glowing. He liked to see her happy, smiling, excited.

"You know," Mimi said, "you added a ton of land when you all bought my place, Bandera."

"Your point?"

She laughed. "That it would almost be *poetic* justice if Malfunction Junction became known for balloon honeymoon retreats."

"I…" He thought about that, liking the sound of the idea, but he needed to dodge his enthusiasm for Holly's sake. He didn't want her to pull back more than she already had. "I think Mason would blow a gasket."

Mimi sighed. "You have a point."

"Fortunately, Marielle offered some land to Holly."

Holly nodded. "She had a pretty place. Very picturesque."

"Cat, cookies…what more do you need to make a home?" he said dryly.

"Sex," Mimi said. "Men usually rank sex right up there with cats and cookies as being the comforts of home."

Holly blushed furiously, which Bandera enjoyed. "Well, now that you mention it…" he said teasingly.

He parked and they got out, walking together to the festival grounds. Holly kept her distance from him, he noted, staying on the other side of Mimi. For now, he'd bide his time, let her work out her feelings of unease.

"This balloon is pretty," she said, stopping abruptly. "A waterfall has been painted on it."

"It is lovely," Mimi agreed. "Get in and try it out."

"We already tried one," Holly said, "and it didn't go so well. Bandera has a fear of heights."

"No, he doesn't," Mimi stated. "I know this for a fact, because he chased Janie—"

"Mimi," Bandera said warningly.

"I'm just saying that if her daddy hadn't gotten out his shotgun, you'd still be up on that roof—"

"I believe I will get in this balloon," Bandera said to keep her from saying more. "Because I didn't learn my lesson the first time."

Mimi laughed. "You never know. This time might be better. I'm going to go find some popcorn. I can smell it cooking. See y'all back here in maybe an hour. Take good notes."

She walked off, smiling. A man in overalls stood by his truck, watching people look at the three balloons he owned. "Howdy," Mimi said.

"Ma'am," he answered, tipping his hat.

"That waterfall balloon is pretty," she told him.

"It's a good one. Bought it a couple years ago from a couple who decided to give up the sport."

"Sport, huh?" She looked over at Bandera and Holly, who were now inside the balloon's basket, talking. "Ever lose one for maybe an hour, in a private place?"

"Could be arranged," he said.

"For a price?"

"Exactly." He grinned. "Those two lovebirds?"

"Actually, no," she said, lowering her voice. "You could think of them more as jailbirds."

His brows raised.

"Yeah, they broke out of a little country jail. Mind you, they're not armed and dangerous, but they did have a little spat with the sheriff's wife over whose peaches were on whose side of the fence."

"I know you're up to trouble, young lady," the

man said with a smile, "but I'm not really interested in your reasons. Show me the cash, and they're as good as lost."

"For a full hour."

"Hell, make it two. I have kids to feed."

Mimi pulled her wallet from her purse. "My brother has this coming to him. He has a fear of heights, you know."

He laughed. "I believe you're getting closer to the truth, but I'm really not interested."

Mimi sighed. "You're almost no fun, you know. All my life, I've been known for being—"

"Mischievous."

She raised her chin. "Have a nice day, sir. Can you point me in the direction of the food tents?"

"Peach pies are piping hot over there," the man said, obviously amused by Mimi. "Shall I send up a snack for those two?"

Mimi glanced over her shoulder. "Nah. Let them live on love."

He laughed.

"So HERE," Holly said, running her hands over the side rails of the basket, "I would tie big ribbons the color of the bride's wedding party, or the couple's favorite colors. Mint and lilac for spring, maybe—"

"Deer and duck head patterns for the guys," Bandera suggested.

She cocked her head. "I never thought about that before. Guy decor."

"Well, yeah. Remember what we liked about Marielle's place? It was comfortable for both sexes. And believe me, if a guy is going to get talked into going up in one of these pear-shaped contraptions, he'd better have some decor that's comforting."

"You know, I don't think you read *Around the World in Eighty Days*," Holly said, laughing at him. "Or saw the movie. Wasn't there recently a billionaire bachelor who took to the skies—"

"Remember, I told you that most gents prefer to keep their boots on the nice hard ground, where matters are as secure as possible," Bandera said. "Possible being the operative..." He hesitated as the balloon shifted, and Holly watched his eyes grow huge. "Wait a minute...are we going up?"

Chapter Eleven

Bandera looked over the side of the basket at the man below him. Six people were gathered round, holding the ropes. "Excuse me," Bandera said. "You're about to lose us."

"Give that burner a little tweak, please," the balloon owner said. "It'll keep you safe until we figure out how to get you back down."

Bandera glanced at Holly. "Welcome to your first experience as an active balloon enthusiast. Give the burner a tweak, whatever that means."

Holly frowned. "It means we'll go up. We don't want that."

"He seems to think it's best." Bandera went over and looked at the burner. "I should have stayed with Mimi's steaming radiator. It was less complicated."

"No, it wasn't," Holly said. "This is less complicated than a bride's hairdo, believe me. Ask him how much of a tweak a tweak is."

"How much of a tweak, sir?" Bandera called over the edge.

"Son, I don't have time to explain," the man yelled back. "If you've ever wanted to be a pilot, this is your chance."

"Really, we just want down," Bandera said.

"I don't," Holly retorted, giving the handle of the burner a small twist. "I see what we did wrong last time. No tweaking."

"Not too much tweaking, please," Bandera said glumly as the flames roared up into the balloon.

Holly smiled. "It's good to see you in a worried state occasionally. You're far too confident. It puts me off."

"No, it doesn't," Bandera said. "You're attracted to it. Women like confidence in a man."

"Oh, is that what we're looking for." Holly gave the burner another tweak.

"Hey! Enough of that!" Bandera grabbed her hand. "They're moving us. Can you feel that?"

They were about fifty feet in the air now, being led to a far corner of the festival grounds. "All the people look very small, but even though it's getting dark, I can still see them," Holly said. "This is cool. When I plan my business, I'm going to make certain that the location is very remote and private." She pulled a brochure from her purse. "Look what I got. An itinerary for a hot air balloon trip in Salzburg, Austria. It's a luxury honeymoon package."

Bandera forgot about his hesitation and gazed over Holly's shoulder. "A balloon ride over Salzburg, Austria, I must admit, tempts even me."

"You would be scared out of your wits."

"Not with an experienced pilot, and this says they have them. 'Late afternoon balloon adventures, skimming over pine trees and meadows tucked away in the foothills of the majestic Alps,'" he read. "Okay, even my brothers, as scattered as their wonderful locations have become, never dreamed of anything this super cool. It may be better than bull riding."

Holly nodded. "It says you stay in a tower built in 1450 by the prince-archbishop of Salzburg as his private hunting and summer residence. Now, see, we can do something nearly as wonderful for the folks who prefer to see Texas rather than Austria."

"Yeah."

Bandera was smelling Holly's hair, and she moved away from him. "Pay attention. We're researching."

They'd stopped, she noticed, and when she peeked over the edge, she saw that the balloon was being tied and anchored in a remote location. "Excuse me," she called, "you'll be wanting to let us down now."

The man in the overalls looked up at her. Cupping

his hands around his mouth, he yelled, "I understand you two are escaped jailbirds."

Holly gasped. "No, sir, we are not! We are law-abiding citizens."

"That's not what she says," he called back loudly as he pointed to a faraway blonde eating ice cream at a picnic table.

"Mimi!" Bandera exclaimed. "That little vixen!"

"What happened?" Holly asked.

"Mimi is having her fun," he replied, turning to stare at the burner. "I guess she rented this balloon to keep us up here for a while. Revenge, no doubt, for every inconsiderate thing Mason and the rest of us ever did to her."

"Aw," Holly said, "I think it's sort of sweet. Except for the jailbird part."

"Trust me, she's having a good giggle over what she's done."

Holly looked the opposite way to keep from smiling.

Bandera turned her back around to face him. "You think this is funny, don't you?"

"Well, it is amusing how she one-upped you," Holly admitted.

"She one-upped you, too," Bandera said.

"No, she didn't. Mimi likes me."

"Hey!" Bandera glared at her. "Mimi's like my little sister!"

"And she's treating you like a brother. This is exactly what sisters do—get their brothers back for all the years of teasing and terrorizing."

"We may have played a joke or two on Mimi, but this is unnecessary. However, if I'm going to spend time aloft, I'm going to spend it doing something I *really* want to do." Bandera pulled Holly into his arms, then sighed with pleasure. "I like holding you. You're a perfect fit for me."

It felt better than she wanted it to and every bit as wonderful as she needed. "I don't see how I can be a perfect fit for you when you're nearly a foot taller than me."

"I like it. You make me feel strong and protective."

She looked up at him. "You make me feel strong and protected. Somehow."

"Good. Between us, we'll beat up on Mimi when she finally lets us down out of this contraption."

"I suppose we could lower the flame on the burner and gently sink to the ground," Holly said.

"What would be the fun in that?" Bandera kissed the top of her head. "We're up here. We might as well…cuddle."

Holly felt her whole body sigh as he kissed her. It was sweet and gentle at first, then heat rushed all over her. "Better stoke it," she said, pulling away. "I want it to stay up."

"It will not go down, I assure you," Bandera said,

reaching under her blouse to stroke her back. "It hasn't needed a lot of stoking around you."

Holly blinked. "Oh, my," she said. "I meant the balloon."

"Don't get all ruffled up, babe," he said with a twinkle in his eye. He moved to the burner, discharging another blast of heat into the balloon.

Holly watched Bandera's big hands as he worked, and his lean body as he turned back toward her. She liked the way his hair fell rakishly over his eyes, and she liked his hat pushed down low on his forehead. In fact, she liked a lot about this man, though she'd been resisting him with everything in her.

And for what? Mason and Mimi resisted each other and that had gotten them nowhere.

Holly didn't want to be nowhere.

"I like being up here with you," she told Bandera.

"I'd like being anywhere with you." His hands slipped along her bare skin, and right then and there, Holly made up her mind.

She wasn't getting out of this balloon, she wasn't putting her feet on the ground, until she had quit resisting him and everything and life itself. "Are you still afraid of heights?" she asked, melting against him.

"I don't particularly care where I am right now, as long as you keep doing that," he said. "It's sort of romantic to be up in a hot air balloon with you starting to take on a little come-hither attitude. And I am a romantic guy, in case you couldn't tell."

She laughed. "Maybe I will put on a little come-hither."

He made a hissing sound and pulled her against him. She could feel parts of his body that were hard—rock hard. "Remember when I met you and asked you to kiss me, and you did?"

"Yeah."

"I liked it." She ran her hands up his chest and wound her arms around his neck.

"I am always happy to oblige you." So he kissed her again, for good measure.

"It was the wildest thing I'd ever done."

He pulled back to look down into her eyes. "Really?"

"Really."

"We've got to loosen you up, babe. Get you wilder."

"I couldn't agree more."

"Hmm, let's see. One of us is going to lose something in this balloon tonight. Either I'm going to lose my fear of heights," he said, "or you're going to lose your fear of rebounding."

She pulled his head down to hers and kissed him on the lips with everything she had. He couldn't miss her meaning. "I had losing something else in mind," she said with a teasing smile. "How's your balance, cowboy?"

WHEN BANDERA AND HOLLY were pulled to earth a couple of hours later, he knew everything had changed. For the worse.

Which he couldn't understand, because they'd made the most explosive love high above the earth that he could have ever imagined. She was a wild woman, and there were moments he'd had to pray that the basket would hold.

As soon as the basket was pulled in, she changed. He wanted to tell the owner to leave them up there for a couple more hours, but that was a fantasy. The reality was that Holly was a different woman on earth. With her fears and insecurities keeping her feet planted somewhere he really couldn't understand.

"Have fun?" Mimi asked with a smile.

"You're in big trouble, little sister," he said, but he could barely manage their normal playful banter.

"How about you?" she asked Holly.

"Very romantic for a business, I think," Holly answered, walking toward the truck.

Mimi glanced at Bandera. "Oops. Did I make everything worse? I was only trying to help."

"No, it was a wonderful gag, and one day, I'll pay you back in spades," he said absently, watching Holly disappear into the crowd. "She loved every minute of it." He shook his head, feeling vaguely sick. "But

I think she's still upset about weddings," he added, "and I guess she's all planned out."

"You asked Holly to marry you?" Mimi asked curiously.

He sighed. "No, that would be too easy." *I make love to her and then let her walk away.*

But going was what she wanted. He'd known that from the moment he'd met her. She wanted a romantic tryst in a hot air balloon, and he'd wanted it, too, and that was that. "I can't ask her to marry me, because she'd say no. Patience is the order of the day."

Mimi looked at him worriedly. "Come on. Let's go home. You're starting to sound like Mason."

"I hope Mason doesn't feel like this," Bandera said, his heart broken, "because it's no fun at all not to be with the woman you love."

"You'll work it out," Mimi said anxiously.

"I don't think so," he replied. "There is no working this out."

BANDERA DROPPED MIMI OFF at her town house and waved at the sheriff, but didn't linger. He had to get Holly home. She seemed to be growing quieter with each passing mile. In another fifteen minutes, she would be totally mute.

He wasn't about to ask her what was wrong. He knew she liked him; he knew their lovemaking had been the real thing.

Something else was bothering her. But she was going to have to come to him this time. She needed to open up and admit she needed him.

He wasn't going to pry her secrets out of her.

So he merely pulled up in front of the address she gave him, a few towns north of Union Junction, and watched as she got out.

"Thank you," she said.

He nodded. "The pleasure was mine."

"It's not you," she said.

"I know." He shrugged. "It doesn't matter."

She seemed surprised by that. "Goodbye, Bandera."

He wasn't about to say goodbye. As he'd warned her, he had plenty of endurance for the chase. Right now, she needed to rest and think. He understood.

Pulling from the driveway, he waved goodbye, leaving her standing in front of a white house with pretty gingerbread scrolls and colorful tulips out front.

As soon as he turned the corner, he stopped his truck and, with hard fingers, dug the tears out of his eyes.

If this was the burden Mason had been carrying around for years, it *stunk*.

Chapter Twelve

One Sunday afternoon a month after the magical night that changed her life, Holly had a visitor.

It was Mimi Cannady.

"Hello," Holly exclaimed, stepping away from the door. "Mimi, it's great to see you! Come in."

"This is a nice home," Mimi said. "It suits you."

"Thank you. Would you care for a lemonade—or maybe a mimosa?"

"A mimosa sounds wonderful." Mimi looked around at the garden-print fabrics on white rattan furniture. "Can I help you make the drinks?"

"No. Sit down. The powder room is down the hall if you want to freshen up."

Holly came back in to find Mimi reading one of her bridal magazines.

"Are you still a wedding planner?"

"No," Holly said, putting the drinks on the glass coffee table. "I sold my business."

"Congratulations! Let's drink to that." Mimi held up her mimosa and they touched them together with a clink. "I like successful businesswomen."

"And speaking of successful women, I bought a piece of Marielle's land."

"Marielle. That's the woman whose bike Mason rode on."

Holly blinked, not knowing how to answer that.

Mimi sighed. "He told me."

"It was a matter of necessity, I think." Holly frowned. "I actually thought she might have had an eye for my cousin Mike."

"That's good to hear." Mimi smiled.

"Did Mason find what he was looking for?" Holly asked.

She shook her head. "Not yet. I think Hawk and Jelly are still on the case, though."

"Have the two of you ever…talked?" Holly asked delicately.

"No, and he doesn't know about Nanette, but the time will be right, hopefully soon, and I'm going to be brave and just say it."

"Oh, dear." Holly had a feeling Mason would probably explode.

"So, have you and Bandera talked?" Mimi asked.

Holly shook her head. "Is that why you're here?"

"No. He doesn't talk to me about things. I just wanted to visit you, make sure you were doing all right." Mimi looked at her guiltily, then shrugged. "Although I will admit that Bandera asked me to come check on you."

Holly smiled softly, pleased that he had. "That's nice of you, Mimi."

"I think he's worried that he might have offended you. He wants to know that you're happy. 'Mimi,' he said—" Mimi mimicked his deep voice "'—even if you find out she married that varmint, that's fine. I just want to know that she's all right.'" Mimi shrugged. "So here I am."

"Oh, no, the varmint and I have little to say to each other. In fact, my mom heard that he and his bride actually divorced. Apparently, his wife caught him with another woman, and that was that."

"Well, let's not waste any pity on them," Mimi said. "Let's talk about going forward with our lives."

Holly raised her eyebrows. "So Bandera sent you to make sure I was all right financially?"

"He said something about wanting to make certain your dreams came true. He said he had a soft spot for hot air balloons and all the romance they signify. And strangely, the other night he was watching a movie with this guy flying around in a balloon. He was quite the daredevil, I must say." Mimi grinned, a light in her eyes. "Bandera said he was studying."

Holly's heart rate speeded up. He was thinking

about her! "I really like him, you know," she told Mimi. "It just wasn't the right time."

"I don't think it ever is. Look at me. Can I lecture you on the way to find the right time? No." Mimi sighed and drank some of her mimosa. "This is delicious. You are clearly cut out to do what you're doing. What more does a bride need in a balloon than a beautiful gown and a mimosa?"

"A hot guy," Holly said.

"I know a few of those," Mimi stated, "and they're mostly part of the same family."

"Okay," Holly said, "I'll bite. What else are you supposed to find out while you're on your errand of inquiry?"

Mimi laughed. "I've achieved his mission. I'm on mine now. Is there anything I can do to persuade you to come for a visit? I think Bandera's heart is broken."

"I can't, Mimi. Fortunately, I know his heart is not broken. I know how these guys operate," Holly said. "They're very protective, very kind, very nurturing."

"All very good things."

"Yes," Holly agreed slowly. "But see it from my perspective. I hadn't lived. I was going from my parents' house to my marriage. And it was a huge mistake. The very day I fled, I met the hottest man I've ever known in my life. Hotter than hot, even. Dream-come-true hot. And," she said, lowering her voice, "I realized I was living my fantasy. With no planning at all. It just happened."

Mimi leaned forward, her blue eyes wide with interest as she reached for her mimosa. "Sounds like a romantic movie to me."

Holly sighed. "But real life intrudes, and I realized that fantasies end eventually."

"Oh." Mimi leaned back. "You know, you should get to know Bandera better. He's pretty fun for a cowboy. And you want some fun in your life, don't you? A girl can't be all work and no play."

"I'm feeling pretty good about my life right now," Holly said. "I've got a new business. I've bought my parents' home—"

"You did?" Mimi looked shocked. "Where are they?"

"On a trip around the world," she reported with a smile. "They said it was time to live life outside the lines. And it's not a big boat, either. It's more like a catamaran. They call occasionally to let me know how they're doing."

Mimi stood. "Be happy, Holly."

"You just got here."

"I know. But I have a youngster at home, and she'll be wanting to play once she gets up from her nap."

"Thank you for coming by."

Mimi nodded. "Congratulations again on your new business." She paused at the front door. "I know you don't want to get hurt again, Holly. I completely understand you feeling the way you do."

Holly felt her smile slip from her face. "The thing with Chuck…it really was awful, Mimi," she said. "It was embarrassing, and sometimes I wonder if that's why my parents sold the house and left to travel the world."

"Of course it's not!"

"I know. But it was terribly humiliating. And upsetting. It shattered my faith in the wonder of marriage."

Mimi handed her a tissue, which Holly took gratefully.

"I didn't want to tell anybody, but of course I can talk to you."

"Yes," Mimi said, "since you're keeping a pretty big secret of mine."

Holly nodded. "My heart turned inside out when I walked in that day and found them. How many weddings had I planned, putting my whole heart into every one? And then it was my turn. I knew after I caught him that he wasn't the right man for me, but it still hurt. And I'm not happy that he's getting divorced. In a way, it would have been better if everyone knew he'd met a woman he loved more than me. Now everyone just knows he's a louse. I don't want to be known for nearly marrying a louse." Holly laughed and wiped her eyes with the back of her hand. "I sound like a nut. You can see that I'm not ready for a man like Bandera."

"But he doesn't care if you sound like a nut, because *he* is nuts," Mimi said. "They all are. It's part of their appeal. Think about it. And maybe after you've finished making the changes in your life that you need to make, you can go have a cup of coffee with him."

Holly shook her head. "I couldn't. I can barely get him out of my mind as it is now."

Mimi blinked. "Isn't that a good thing?"

"Not when you've had hot sex in a balloon," Holly said. "You tend to obsess about how great it was."

"Ohh," Mimi said. "Is that why he's watching that movie with the guy in the balloon?" She giggled. "You two have got to stop longing for each other. Trust me, a bed works just fine." Laughing, she hugged Holly. "I'll tell him you're fine…and thinking about him," she said.

"Don't you dare!" Holly squeaked.

"Holly, I am the woman who paid money to get you stranded in the sky with Bandera," Mimi stated with a wink. "But I promise not to say a word."

"Thank you," Holly said. "It's better this way."

Mimi turned to walk away, then slowly turned back. "Can I just say one thing, between us girls?"

She nodded.

"I hate to see you make the same mistake I made. Fear is a bad thing to give in to."

"I know. And yet I feel safer on my own."

"I understand," Mimi said. "Letting someone into your life is an adventure in itself."

BANDERA THOUGHT AGAIN about the note Mimi had left him yesterday, his heart tearing in two.

> Holly's fine. She sold her business, bought her parents' house and a piece of Marielle's land. She said to tell you hi. Love, Mimi

How could he feel so much for her when she felt nothing for him?

Deep in thought, he rubbed a saddle, looking at the sheen on the leather, before he realized that two kids were looking up at him. "Hey, Kenny, Minnie," he said. "What are you two rascals doing up at this hour?"

"We wanted to pet the horses before we left. Mom's taking us to buy sparklers," Minnie said.

"Sparklers, huh? That sounds like fun."

Kenny put his hand over the rail to pet the horse. He looked up at Bandera. "Mom says she hopes you bring your girlfriend to the Fourth of July picnic."

Bandera rubbed his chin, recognizing well-wishing from Kenny's mother, Olivia. "I don't actually have a girlfriend, Kenny."

Minnie's eyes went round. "Do you want one?"

Bandera gave his horse a long brush with his palm. "I do."

Minnie wrinkled her nose. "I like this boy at school. I wish he'd just say hi. But he never does. Why do boys not like to say hi?" Her mouth turned down. "He stole my prettiest ribbon on the last day of school."

Kenny nodded. "Right from her hair. He did it on the playground. I saw him."

Bandera smiled ruefully. "I don't have the answer to that question. I can guess, though. Sometimes boys don't say hi because they're scared."

"That's dumb," Minnie declared.

"Yeah." He laughed, thinking that even men were sometimes scared of women. "It's something you might have to get used to, though."

"Guys should say hello."

"And therein lies the first hurdle for men and women. Who should say hi first? Who should call whom?" He ruffled her hair. "Truthfully, I think it's a good sign he stole your ribbon." Bandera had a few mementos from Holly, and he wasn't giving them back.

"You do? Mom said she'd talk to his mother and make him give it back if I wanted her to."

"I think he might have wanted something to remember you by over the summer." Bandera laughed as he sat down on a barrel and looked at both kids. "How about this? I'll ask a lady I know if she'll come to the picnic to meet you and to be with us."

"Good," Minnie said. "She probably wishes you would ask."

"Well, I don't know about that, but a man's got to try."

Minnie and Kenny nodded. Kenny puffed out his chest, trying to be manly.

"And I will take you to the store myself," Bandera said, "and help you choose a ribbon, Minnie, and a hatband or pinwheel, whatever you want, Kenny, for the Fourth of July. But let's tell Mom it's okay for your friend to keep the ribbon."

"Did you ever steal a girl's ribbon?" Kenny asked.

"Come on," Bandera said, walking from the barn with his niece and nephew. "If I tell you I did, you'll be stealing ribbons with the best of them."

"No. I'm just going to say hi to girls. That's what Minnie says I should do."

"And you should always listen to your sister. She's very smart."

"We're going now," Minnie said. "Don't forget to ask the lady. Otherwise you won't have a partner for the three-legged race."

"Oh, boy. That's right." Bandera waved as they ran toward their house on the ranch property, with its windmill turning slowly behind.

"I'm not sure how much Holly would enjoy being tied to me at the ankle, but I suppose I should be brave," he murmured thoughtfully. Then he looked at the note from Mimi again. No sign in there that Holly wanted to see him.

He sat on a rail and contemplated his position as he looked at the sunshine flooding the landscape. Why did a woman give a man her virginity and then disappear? Had that been just a fling? Obviously, they had both been aware of the romance of the moment, but he was certain she had wanted *him* just as much as he'd wanted her.

He hated to think she might have been taking some revenge upon the memory of her ex. "Hell hath no fury like a woman scorned," he said to himself. "Or something like that." But he knew that kind of dramatic quote really didn't fit Holly. She was far too gentle.

The only way to discuss how she felt was to find out for himself. He couldn't snatch a ribbon from her hair, or tease her out of her panties. She was moving on with her life, and if he didn't quit being a chicken and find out how she felt, the opportunity might be lost to him forever.

TWO HOURS LATER, Bandera sat in front of Holly's home. She wasn't there. He knew because the newspaper was on the front lawn and the porch light was off. Twilight was falling in the sleepy neighborhood, and a light mist made the streetlights glow. He could see her being happy here in her parents' home. Holly had said she was looking for safe.

But she was also looking for excitement in her life, or she wouldn't have sold her business and opted to try something new. Or gone on a balloon ride with him. All very risky.

There were two ways he could try to win her heart. One, safely. He could walk to the front door and ring the bell, hand her some flowers and invite her to the picnic.

Safe.

Or he could be outrageous and fun.

"Flip a coin, Bandera," he said. "Everything's hanging in the balance." What did a woman *really* want? It wasn't as simple as Minnie yearning for the boy she liked to say hello to her. Love between a man and a woman went deeper than that; it was based on two halves fitting together to make a whole, where needs were anticipated and satisfied.

Risky or safe. What did a woman who lived in the house she'd grown up in and yet made love in a balloon really want?

"Hey," said a voice by his ear.

He sat up straight, his heart jumping. "Hey, Holly."

She glanced inside his truck. "What are you doing?"

He gazed solemnly at her, drinking in her fresh beauty and the slight smile on her lips. "Having a debate."

"With who?"

"Myself."

"Oh. I thought there had to be two people for a debate."

This was not the dramatic romance he'd been debating. "I don't have anyone to argue with. It's just me, myself and I."

"Oh. Well, my neighbor called me down at the flower shop and told me there was a cowboy sleeping in his truck in front of my house. She wanted to know if she should come shoo you off." Her eyes twinkled at him.

"I'm glad you came to do it yourself," he said. "I wouldn't want to be shooed by a stranger."

"Bandera. Would you like to come in?"

An invitation! *Stay cool, Bandera. Follow her lead.* Getting out of the truck, he said, "I hear you've been busy."

"Yeah, I have. It was sort of sweet of you to send Mimi to check on me."

He followed her inside the house. "Sort of?"

"Yeah." Holly went into the kitchen and he looked around at the flowered wallpaper and yellow-covered chairs. "I know Mimi gave you the update."

"Yes. Proud owner of a new home and business. Congratulations."

"And I've got the bubbly." She poured him a beer. "Michelob, but bubbly."

"Suits my taste just fine." He drank the beer gratefully, hoping to chase away some of his nerves. She looked more beautiful than he remembered.

"I was thinking about our balloon experience the other day," she said, handing him a plate of cheese and crackers.

"Were you?" He didn't think now was the time to mention that he thought about it maybe a thousand times a day.

She smiled. "I'm really glad it happened. Thank you for making it so beautiful."

Oh, God, he was going to die. She was writing him off. A thank-you was a certain goodbye. In fact, she was probably planning to join a nunnery. He had to act quickly. "My niece and nephew want you to come to our family Fourth of July picnic so you can be my three-legged-race partner."

Now if that wasn't romance, he didn't know what was.

She didn't say anything. But she was smiling.

"Do you like three-legged races?" he asked.

"I don't know. But I'm into trying new experiences these days."

He gulped. "Me, too."

"I wish I'd met you at a different time in my life, Bandera," she said softly.

Uh-oh, that didn't sound good. "No time like the present, I always say. Some things can't be timed. Actually, the only things I can think of that are successfully timed are boiled eggs and chocolate chip cookies."

She looked down at her fingers, but he saw the smile on her face.

"What is it, exactly?" he asked. "Between you and me?"

Her eyes widened. Bandera tensed inside. Well, that was the combination of risky and safe he'd been looking for, he guessed; even Minnie would have to approve of his direct approach.

"I don't know," she said. "I want to make love to you again. I think about it all the time."

He could be very obliging. Wherever she wanted, whenever she wanted. Right now, the kitchen floor would do just fine for hot, sweaty sex.

But he knew that's not what she wanted, either.

On the other hand, a man couldn't go around snatching ribbons instead of showing his true feelings. He stood, grabbing her around the waist and pulling her against him.

"What are you doing?" she asked.

"Measuring you for the three-legged race. I aim to win, and I need to know if we fit together."

"If we can make love standing up in a hot air balloon, I think we can run tied together at the ankle," she said.

"Oh, you just gave yourself away," he said, sweeping her up into his arms. "I'm going to make love to you, and when I'm done, I want you to say that you're coming to our family picnic. You need to get to know the rest of the Jeffersons." He pulled off his belt. "You need to get to know me better."

Bending down, he tied the belt around both their ankles. She started to laugh, pulling at his hair. "This is not how a man romances a woman. I'm sure it's not. I never saw this in any of my bridal magazines."

He put his arm around her shoulder so they were connected. "You've been reading all the wrong periodicals. Run," he said. "To your bedroom. Or wherever your little heart desires to make love this time."

She stared up at him.

"Well, go," he said. "You have to take some initiative in this relationship. It's part of my plan to break you free from all your pent-up worries and fears. One foot in front of the other now," he said.

A pretty blush spread over her cheeks. "Bandera, I can't run with you."

"Why? You want me to do all the work in this relationship? So far I have, you know."

Her lips pursed.

"I want you to want me, Holly. Or you can take us apart. It's only a standard belt buckle, it's not a wedding ring."

She bit her lip, then said, "Hold on tight, cowboy. I'm pretty sure you can't handle heights." And she headed up the stairs, dragging him. They stumbled, and he couldn't keep up with her, so they lay on the staircase, kissing as if they would never stop.

"I will take off the belt, seeing as how I had to drag you up here," Holly said. "It was like dragging a two-hundred-pound sack of rice. I don't think we're going to win the race at your family picnic."

Once the belt was released, he pressed her back onto the carpet-covered steps.

"Good to see you at least won't lag behind like a broken-down mule. I missed you," he said. "I don't like you playing hard to get." He gave her a little slap on the bottom as he pulled off her jeans.

"And I don't like you being so easy to run off," she said, slapping him on the rear end as she pulled his jeans off. "I thought you said you had *endurance*."

He tore off her blouse, holding it to his nose to smell her fragrance. "On the other hand, I like how you're not desperate," he said.

She squatted over him in her sweet little pink-and-white-dotted thong to pull off his boots, which he appreciated. "On the other hand, I like how *you* gave me time to clear my head. I really couldn't jump from one relationship to another. It would have been weird."

"And what would we have told the neighbors?" he asked, tossing her shoes to the floor and undoing her brassiere. "Miss Bride on the Fly."

"Oh, my gosh! My neighbor who called to tell me

there was a cowboy outside my house will be looking to see if you're still here and if I'm safe!"

He held her down when she tried to escape. "We'll invite her to the wedding, when you ask me nicely to marry you."

She gave him a light punch on the chest, so he tore her thong off of her. "So much beauty," he said, "and it's all mine."

"So much pigheadedness, and I'm stuck with it," she said, moving to be on top of him.

"That's all right, Miss Independent. You be on top, since you like being in charge, and I'll just be happy." He ran his palms over her breasts, squeezing the nipples lightly. "You are the sexiest woman I have ever seen."

She tugged off his boxers and gave a thumbs-up to his erection, before she settled over him. "You're definitely the most caveman-man I have ever met." She slid down him, and he held his breath, putting his hands on her hips so that he could enjoy the feeling of her throwing caution to the wind.

"Let's always have fun," he said, flipping her over so that he could get farther inside her. He kissed her so hard he thought he would explode from the heat and the hardness and all the feelings that she called forth from somewhere deep in his soul.

"Crazy," she said, crossing her legs up over his back so she could hold him tight. "Let's always be crazy."

"Crazy works for me," he said, thrusting inside her just to see her eyes close as she strained for pleasure. "Holly, you're magic."

He touched his finger to the hot spot between them, lightly massaging her pleasure zone until she cried out, then he rocked against her until she yelled his name. He kissed her, claiming her, before whispering in her ear, "You are always going to yell my name just like that."

Pleasure so hot swept over him that he stopped thinking. When it was over and his mind came back to him, he realized Holly was holding him tighter than anyone had ever held him in his life.

Almost as if she was afraid he wasn't real.

Chapter Thirteen

Holly held Bandera tightly, knowing she had to let go but wanting to lie like this forever. With him. Nothing in her life had prepared her for the beauty of passion. He made her happy; he made her feel excitement.

"Hey," he said, looking down at her.

She finally released him and gave him a smile. "Hey, yourself," she said.

He kissed her neck. "Standing up or at an incline?"

"Balloon or stairs? Too hard to choose." She got up and began putting her clothes back on. "So much for me being the girl who waited until the altar."

Bandera laughed, a throaty growl that raised goose pimples on her skin. He pulled her back down and took her thong from her before she had a chance to get it over both feet. "This has polka dots. Nice of you to remember my favorite pattern."

"I didn't. And they're pink. As I recall, that wasn't your favorite color."

"No, but polka dots are good luck."

"I didn't know you were superstitious."

The smile melted off his face. "Oh, no. You shouldn't have said that."

Holly sat up. "Said what?"

"The *S* word!"

She giggled. "Superstition?"

"Shh!" He sat up, his brows furrowed.

"Bandera, you're creeping me out," she said. "I can handle making love in a stairwell, but polka dots and superstitions make you almost too wild for me."

"I was going to be the first man to fall in love without invoking the family superstition," he told her. "I haven't *hurt* anything."

"You're into that kind of stuff?" She got up, snatching her underwear from him. "I'm into crazy. But no pain."

"Holly!" Bandera began dressing, too. "Every man in my family has hurt something when he met the woman for him."

She smiled. "Maybe I'm not the one." Dressed now, she went down the stairs into the kitchen. "I wouldn't want to hurt you, anyway. That's sick."

"No, it's superstition. And it works for us. It began with Frisco Joe." Bandera followed her around the kitchen, trying to be helpful as she set up a tray of veggies, but really he just got in the way. She slapped his hand.

"Ow," he said.

"There, I've hurt you. Does that count?"

"I don't think so. It's not significant pain." He looked at her funny, and Holly's heart turned over.

"Bandera, I realize you're not the typical man, but superstitions make me nervous. I'm not a rabbit's foot kind of girl."

"That's it," he said. "You're right. We're not rabbit's foot kind of people."

Holly hugged him. "Now see how strange that sounded. Already you're rubbing off on me."

"I want *you* to rub off on *me*," he said, kissing her. "I'm pretty certain there's more to like about you than not."

"How do you know that?" she asked softly. "I have never understood what it was that made you so sure of everything."

"I don't know. Most of the time, I just go on instinct."

"No planning."

"None at all."

She pulled away, looking up at him, wondering what he was really thinking. "You know, we're completely opposite."

"Nothing boring about that."

But he didn't sound as convinced as he once had,

and Holly couldn't help feeling that a little of the magic had just blown away.

BANDERA WAVED AT Holly's neighbor, who was staring out through her curtains, then got in his truck, wishing he felt better about the evening. Holly was his woman, he knew it in his bones.

And yet something was missing.

"Mason," he said, a couple of hours later when he walked inside the kitchen of the main house at Malfunction Junction. "What do you remember most about Mom and Dad?"

Mason looked up from an apple he was cutting. "That Mom was always teasing Dad. She could make him laugh even when he was tired."

So laughter made a successful relationship. Bandera and Holly laughed together.

"How's Holly?" Mason asked.

"She's fine. And she's coming to the Fourth of July picnic."

"Excellent. I'll tell Last to put an extra plate on the picnic table." Mason flipped a piece of apple his way, and Bandera caught it with his mouth.

"You're good at catching things," Mason said. "Only you and Last can do that successfully."

"Speaking of catching things," Bandera said, "can you catch cold feet?"

"Hell, no," Mason said. "There's no such thing."

Bandera stared at his brother. "Then what the hell is your problem?"

Mason stopped chopping, his frown deep. "What's that supposed to mean?"

Bandera ground his teeth, wanting to tell his brother the truth about Mimi, and the truth about their baby. But he knew it wasn't his place, even if Mason was so stubborn he would never ease up enough for Mimi to tell him. "It means you've got the worst case of cold feet I've ever seen."

"I don't know what you're talking about."

"Mimi," Bandera said. "Everybody in this house walks on eggshells around you when it comes to Mimi, but it's time something got said."

"No," Mason said, "it's definitely not time for you to harangue me about anything."

Bandera set his jaw. "I nearly proposed today."

His brother seemed surprised. "Good for you."

"Only I couldn't," Bandera continued, "because I thought about pain. And superstition. And why our family lives at a place called Malfunction Junction." He took a deep breath. "Then I realized none of us is ever going to lead a normal life until your head is screwed on straight."

"Have you lost your mind?" Mason's face turned red. "Do you want me to open up a can of whup-ass on you—"

"Hey," Last said, coming into the kitchen. "Are

we having another close, enjoyable family dinner tonight?"

"Shut up," Mason said, reaching for him. "I'm sick of your smart mouth."

"Hey, what did I say?" Last demanded, edging away.

Crockett came in, nearly catching Mason's swing. "What in the name of Sadie Grace is going on? Mason, cool it, dude."

"I don't want to cool it," Mason said. "Y'all have been wanting me to express myself, and now I'm ready."

The last four bachelors of Malfunction Junction began ducking and dodging and throwing light punches as they circled the kitchen. Bandera reached out to test Mason's reflexes with a little tap to his chest, just a small one, but Mason kicked out with his boot, catching him in the ankle.

Bandera went down, and the last thing he remembered as he fell to the floor was Holly's face when he'd left her.

She'd been scared—and for the first time, he had been, too.

"BANDERA," a voice said. "Bandera!"

The voice was small and sweet and reminded him of someone. Someone he liked a lot and who made him feel good. Slowly, he opened his eyes. Holly sat beside his bed.

"Hey, Holly." The pain in his skull was piercing. "You finally came to me. I told you you would."

She breathed a sigh of relief. "Well, he didn't knock any of the nonsense out of you."

"No one knocked me," Bandera said.

"Mason said he did, and a sorrier brother you have never seen. He's moping around the house. He thinks he nearly killed you."

"Hmm. I can't remember." Bandera smiled at her, and it was a loopy kind of smile.

"Let me go get Doc. He wanted to see you as soon as you woke up."

"Why do I have to see Doc?"

"Because you hit your head on the corner of the stove. Crockett wanted to take you to the hospital, but Mason said it was too far, and Doc could get here quicker." Holly slipped from the room and went down the hall. "Mason? Doc? Bandera's awake."

"Good," Doc said. Holly followed him nervously. The sight of Bandera laid up in bed was difficult to bear. When Last had called and asked her to come out, she had immediately jumped in her car and driven to the ranch. He'd said there'd been an incident and Bandera had gotten hurt. By the tone in his voice, she knew Bandera was really hurt, more than his superstition called for.

Doc examined Bandera's eyes and checked his skin.

"I still think he needs a scan," he told Mason. "I don't know that this is your garden-variety coldcocking."

"I don't need a scan," Bandera said. "I'm fine." He smiled at Holly. "You're pretty."

"Oh, boy," Mason said as Last and Crockett came to stand beside him.

"That was mushy even for Bandera the poet," Crockett said.

"Poet?" Bandera frowned. "I'm not a poet."

"A little look-see by the city docs can't hurt, Mason," Doc said. "Your bell is a bit rung, Bandera."

"I'm just tired." Bandera closed his eyes before slowly opening them again. "Don't leave," he said to Holly. "You're the only one looking at me like you know me."

She reached out to hold his hand, which made him smile.

"I don't know," Doc said. "It'd be best if he had his condition—"

"No," Bandera said. "I probably just need something to eat."

"How about chocolate chip cookies?" Holly asked. "I was baking when Last called, so I brought some with me."

Bandera opened his eyes and smiled at her. "I know you, and you are someone I feel very comfortable with."

She sighed. "You might not be comfortable in an

emergency room," she said, "but at least you'd have better medicine than cookies."

"I'm staying here." Bandera's mouth flattened, and his face turned a bit pale.

"All right," Mason said, then he, Doc, Last and Crockett filed out silently.

Holly looked at Bandera. "You're too stubborn."

He closed his eyes, then opened them again. "When the bees quit buzzing in my head, I want to marry you."

"Why?"

"I don't know why. I just know I do."

Holly shook her head. "Bandera, you and I agreed to do a three-legged race together, and that required major commitment on both our parts. I don't think we can go from a three-legged race to a marriage proposal."

"Go ahead. Ask me."

She smiled. "I can't. The man asks the woman."

He moaned, touching his head.

"All right." Holly took a deep breath. "Bandera, will you marry me?"

He grinned from ear to ear. "I always knew you had it in you, Holly." Pulling her into the bed beside him, he kissed her deeply. "I'm crazy about you, girl."

She beat on his arm. "You were *faking*."

"I was not. I have a helluva headache and I'm going to whip Mason's ass when I can see straight. But the one thing I see just fine is you." He kissed her palms and then each of her eyes. "And you're good medicine for me. I loved hearing you ask me to marry you, in that sweet little voice."

"Let me up," she said. "I'm going to concuss you myself."

"My little firecracker," he said. "All these fireworks in bed just in time for the Fourth of July. And you know what would make me have a one hundred percent recovery?"

"Bandera!"

He laughed. "Some of those chocolate chip cookies you brought."

"Go ahead, have your laugh," she said. "You're the one lying in a bed with your head splitting. I'm feeling no pain whatsoever."

He grabbed her fingers. "One day, my little wedding planner, I'm going to make love to you in a bed, in a traditional nod to marital bliss, and you're going to think heaven is in a standard four-poster. We've made love, and you know that on some level you belong to me."

She jerked her hand away. "I take back my proposal. You're a faker."

He let go of her, and she made her escape, though part of her wished she was still with him, snuggled up next to his strength.

The realistic side of her knew she had to leave. She was falling for him.

So she left the bedroom and went to the kitchen. She put the cookies on a plate, then took them into the den to Last. "I think the patient is coming around. Here's the medicine he requested."

"Aren't you taking them to him?" Last asked. "He seems to respond better to you."

"Actually, I'm not. I need to get back home."

"Oh," Last said. "It's like that, is it?"

"Yes," Holly said. "It's like that. But thank you for calling me to let me know he was hurt. I don't think the superstition worked the way he thought it would."

"Superstition?" Last asked.

"The one about pain and injury."

"Oh, that's just a crock of sh— I mean, that's bull malarkey," Mason said. "I've never been hurt."

"Neither have I," Last said.

"Yeah, and neither of you have ever been in love," Crockett said. "I believe in the Curse of the Broken Body Parts, and I stay away from painful occurrences linked to women."

These men were committed bachelors, every one of them. They honestly believed that they had to experience pain to make it to the altar. That love was inherently painful in some way. She understood. She'd been through a painful experience at the altar herself.

Holly walked out of the ranch house, sorry to be going but knowing that she had to leave.

Chapter Fourteen

The Fourth of July dawned hot and steamy, but Bandera didn't care. Today he was going to be tied at the ankle to Holly Henshaw.

And then he was going to pop the Big Question.

He'd had about a week to think about it, as he'd been stuck in the house, courtesy of Doc's orders. Really stupid, he kept telling Doc. There was nothing wrong with him. The pain was worth every bit of the gain he was planning.

There were picnic tables set up, and pinwheels blew on every table, stuck in pots of geraniums. Big flags hung off the porch. The mailbox wore a big bow, and even the dog had a giant red-white-and-blue bandanna tied around its neck.

Bandera smelled barbecue cooking. Mason had gone all out for this occasion. Now that so many kids were on the ranch and in the family, he was inclined to be very decorative during the holidays.

It gave the brothers a reason to return home, if their kids were begging them to visit Uncle Mason.

Mimi was there with Nanette. Bandera took a deep breath, hating secrets. He would know everything about Holly, and she would know everything about him.

He watched Nanette run across a field after Kenny and Minnie. Glancing at his watch, he thought about the surprise he had for Holly.

If she came.

She would. He'd left a message on her phone yesterday, and she hadn't called to say she had other plans.

She hadn't called at all.

A chill swept over him. "I think I'll mosey to town," he said to Last, who was walking by with a huge bowl of macaroni salad.

"Gotcha," Last said. "Valentine and the little one are bringing some sugar cookies from her bakery today, but would you mind…hey, Bandera. You've got company."

He wheeled around. Holly was walking toward him, carrying five large Mylar balloons and what looked like a cake. "Howdy!" he said. He rushed to meet her, relieved that she'd kept her word. "You brought me a present!"

"No," Holly said. "I brought the children balloons. Did you tell me there were five children here? If not, I need to go get some more balloons."

"This is plenty. It can be a centerpiece for the dessert table." He drank in the sight of her. "I didn't think you'd show."

"And miss the chance to be tied to your ankle?"

He helped her put the cake down, but not without sticking his finger in it. "Oops. Accident." He licked his finger happily.

"Yeah, right." Holly rolled her eyes.

"Homemade," he said. "Lemon cake, French vanilla icing."

"Strawberry filling, too. But don't stick your finger into the middle of the cake, okay?"

He grinned. "You really are good at everything, aren't you?"

"Not wedding planning," she said. "I just found out the business I sold, Weddings By Holly, had such a bad reputation because of my disastrous wedding that the buyer changed the name." She tried to smile, but embarrassment prevented it. "I would have liked to go out with a bang."

Pulling her close, he said, "Listen, I bumped my head, so I got enough bang for all of us, okay? You can make a success out of marriage later. Focus on the honeymoon business. It's all about the balloons."

She smiled. "You are making me feel better."

"Good. Look to the future. And here's Valentine," Bandera said. "You and Valentine should have a lot to talk about. She's just opened her own business, Baked Valentines."

"Congratulations," Holly said. "It's great to own your own business, isn't it?"

"I think so. I'm still a little nervous." Valentine smiled at Bandera. "But I'm very grateful to the Jefferson boys for backing me and helping me get started."

"Really? And I thought the backing I received was special," she said, thinking of the thousand dollars Bandera had given her.

"Oh, that was quite different." Bandera chuckled, then changed the subject. "Valentine and Last have a child. In fact, this would be the little darling," he said, scooping up the little girl as she tried to hide behind Valentine's skirt. "This is Annette. Our precious ladybug."

The little girl blushed and hid her face against Bandera's shoulder.

Valentine smiled. "It was nice to meet you, Holly. Let me know if I can send over some baked goods for your new business. We can do balloon shapes."

"Oh, now that's an idea," Holly said. "Thank you, Valentine."

"See you at the races," she said, taking Annette from Bandera and heading toward the other kids.

They could hear the happy laughter of children. "Last is with them, I think," Bandera said.

"Let me get this straight," Holly said. "Last and Valentine have a child, but—"

"No. They never got married. It doesn't always work out, you know."

"Yes, I do."

He pulled her close to him. "But we love children here. And family. Holly, I realize we're different from a lot of families, but we stay with our friends through thick and thin." Touching her face, he said, "You know you want me."

She laughed and slapped his hand away. "I don't know. Marrying a man from Malfunction Junction would probably not help my reputation. Weddings by Holly, Divorce By Golly."

"Very tacky, I agree. You did lots of weddings. They didn't all end up badly, did they?"

"It just took mine falling apart for the name to stick, I suppose."

"You didn't even get married." He walked away from her a few steps. "Well, come on, Miss By Golly."

"Where are we going?"

"I think it's time for the three-legged race."

"Do you think you should do that in your condition?" Holly asked.

"I wouldn't miss this chance to show you that my family is full of good old-fashioned fun." Bandera grinned. "And it may be the most tying-down of you I ever get to do. I wore an extra-thick belt today."

She shook her head. "Oh, no, cowboy. I brought a special belt just for you." And she pulled a long ribbon from her pocket, white with lots of tiny black polka dots.

"You are the woman of my dreams," he said. "You have no idea how much Minnie is going to approve of this."

"Minnie?"

"Yes. She lost a favorite ribbon recently to a little boy on the playground and hasn't quite forgiven him for the dent in her collection."

Holly smiled. "This should help."

"And every time I see this ribbon in her hair, I'll think of you. You're such a dotty lass."

"I'm ignoring that because you have suffered a slight head injury." She bent down and began tying the ribbon so that the two of them were joined together.

"Almost as good as a wedding ring," Bandera said. "Two become one, and all that."

"Or possibly we are the two-headed monster. We'll find out. Please try not to lag behind," Holly instructed. "I intend to win this race."

"Minnie and Kenny are racing against us," he warned her. "They're far more flexible."

"Focus, Bandera," she said. "Together now. Get into the rhythm."

"All I do is think about sex around you," he said, leaning on her so he could feel her body tight against his. "Everything you say and do makes me think about the next fun place I can have you."

"This is a family affair. Keep it G-rated," Holly said. "If we don't make a good showing, I'm blaming it on your lack of concentration."

He forced himself to think about nothing but walking in sync. But she felt so good tucked up under his arm. *This is what I want for the rest of my life. I don't want to be like Mason. I don't want a sideways thing like what Last has. I want this woman, and I want it to be the marriage she's always wanted.*

Bandera watched as several pairs of his brothers and family friends gathered at the starting line. Sheriff Cannady was there to call the start; Shoeshine Johnson would call the finish. Minnie and Kenny were paired, as were Frisco Joe and his wife, Annabelle, who'd come in from the Texas wine country. Laredo and Katy, Hannah and Ranger, Fannin and Kelly, Tex and Cissy—everybody was there for the fun. Last had paired up with Helga the housekeeper, and Valentine was paired with Crockett.

"I hope you're fast," Bandera said to Holly.

"I hope you don't slow us down," she retorted.

"On your mark, get set…go!" the sheriff hollered.

They all took off at an awkward pace, lumbering along as best they could for people who weren't used to being strapped together at the ankle. Holly was laughing so hard he didn't think she was going to be able to keep running. Finally, Bandera picked her up and hauled her toward the finish line.

They were winning, he was happy to see. It was great to be able to outrun his brothers. Holly was hanging on for dear life, squealing, "Go, Bandera!" and he was going for all he was worth. That is, until he stepped in a gopher hole or some other rodent burrow and lost his balance, falling forward, with Holly's weight pulling him that much faster as they landed in a heap on the ground.

"Bandera!" Holly gave him a little pop on the shoulder, laughing. "Get up! Keep running! We nearly won!"

He was glad to hear it, but she was lying on his leg, which felt a bit different than normal, mostly because of the pain shooting up his calf. "You can take off the polka dots now," he said. "I'm done with that pattern."

"What?" She leaned close, their ankles twisting together in the ribbon noose. He moaned, and she moved his hat back. "Are you all right?"

"Untie me, and I'll be fine."

She did, quickly.

Minnie and Kenny skidded over after they'd captured first place. They bent down, examining Bandera carefully.

"What are you doing?" Kenny asked.

"Counting ants," Bandera said between gritted teeth. "You've heard it's not a picnic until the ants are invited?"

"Are you…hurt?" Minnie asked.

"I believe I am." Bandera closed his eyes. "Kenny, will you ask Doc to step over here, please, son?"

Minnie leaned close to his ear. "You look like Uncle Calhoun when he was stretched out on the ground after falling from the tree. He ought not have been up on that ladder fixing bird feeders."

"He was just helping you kids out," Bandera said, looking into her eyes.

"Yeah, Uncle Bandera," Minnie said, "but you know what this means."

Holly leaned in close. "I know what it means."

Minnie said, "You do?"

"Mmm. It's the curse. Or superstition. Bandera's going to get married."

Minnie grinned, and Bandera smiled wanly. "You don't believe in the superstition."

"No, but I believe in you," she said. "Bandera, do you remember when I told you that the man asked the woman?"

"Yeah. I thought you were such an independent lass, with your woman-owned business and your house ownership. I didn't know how you could not understand it didn't matter who did the asking."

"I understand that now that I know the real you," Holly said, "so I'm asking."

Doc came to stand over him, squatting down to gently probe his leg. "Ankle?"

"Think so. But my heart's not broken anymore," Bandera said happily. "I'm getting a wedding proposal."

All his brothers and their wives and children were now standing around them, some still connected at the ankles.

"Are you accepting?" Doc asked curiously. "'Cuz Hawk just called and he and Jelly are on the way in. We could have a bang-up wedding, right here, with sparklers and all."

"I'm accepting," Bandera said. "But just so the traditionalist in you will be satisfied, Holly Henshaw, amazing wedding planner, will you do me the honor of becoming my wife?"

"I will," she said, throwing her arms around his neck. "I love you, Bandera Jefferson. I'm so glad you have excellent endurance."

"Even though he does step in gopher holes," Kenny said.

But Holly didn't care. She was too busy being kissed by her new fiancé.

"Good thing you said yes," Minnie said. "I was kinda wondering what Uncle Bandera was going to do with that pretty balloon if you said no."

"What?" Holly looked up at the little girl, and all the smiling faces of her new family around her. "What balloon?"

"That one," Minnie said, pointing.

Holly looked up to see a giant balloon floating overhead, the beautiful waterfall balloon where they'd first made love. She squealed with joy and surprise. "Bandera!" Tightening her arms around his neck, she said, "Can you get up?"

"I think so."

Everybody helped him, and he stood, testing his ankle. But not for long, because his wife-to-be tucked herself under his arm, bracing him, so that together they could walk, not run, toward their future.

"I love you, Holly," he said. "We're taking that balloon trip in Salzburg for our honeymoon. We need to know everything about our new occupation." And then he kissed her, long and deep, holding her close, as the balloon gently floated overhead. "And don't worry. This is one wedding that is certain to go off without a hitch!"

Holly laughed, looking up into her groom's eyes. "You're just the right combination of traditional and outrageous. Being married to you is going to be so much fun. I'm so glad to be a Malfunction Junction bride!"

He enclosed her in his arms, and together they turned to look toward their family, laughing as they saw everybody waving at them, some holding sparklers that sparked and Kenny and Minnie holding up a sign that read Uncle Bandera's Balloon Rides for Kids.

"I don't think they got the part about it being a honeymoon business," he told Holly, laughing.

"It's something to consider," she said, smiling up at him. "An entrepreneur should always consider *all* the ways to increase business. Now about those kids…"

He grinned and ushered Holly toward the waterfall balloon, which had just landed. "Anytime you like, babe," he said. "Happy Independence Day."

Bandera had set her heart totally free.

Epilogue

Bandera would not be satisfied until he'd given Holly a traditional ring, a traditional wedding and a traditional honeymoon. Not to mention traditional lovemaking.

"I like the little cabin you decorated," Holly told him as they held hands, waiting for Hawk to come and marry them in front of all their family and friends. Two days wasn't long when planning a wedding, but then again, he didn't want to give Holly a *chance* to plan another wedding.

That was a waste of time, considering they were already married, in his mind. Plus he knew Holly wanted to be swept off her feet.

Fortunately, the ladies at the Union Junction salon were willing to help. They took Holly under their wing, helping with hair, shoes and a lovely wedding gown.

It was white and long with pretty flowers and sequins scattered over the skirt. And they didn't pile her hair high and put twinkly things in it, they left it loose and long, just the way he liked it. She wore a circlet of baby's breath in her hair, with satin ribbons trailing down the back.

She looked like a fairy princess.

"I have a little surprise for you," she said. "It's under my gown."

He raised his brows, appreciating whatever lay in store for him. "I'd love a hint."

"Lacy. White. Tiny black polka dots. We have on matching ensembles. Do the words Victoria's Secret help you?"

A grin lit his face. Bandera hugged Holly close to him. "I love my black silk boxers, especially the white polka dots."

"I find there's a peaceful repetition in the pattern," she said with a smile.

He held her to him. "I never saw it that way before."

Hawk and Jellyfish pulled up at that moment, their faces inscrutable. If the sight of all the people, the hot air balloon waiting for a wedding getaway, and a bride didn't shake them, Bandera supposed nothing would.

Hawk grinned at Holly. "I see you found your destiny."

"Yes." She smiled up at Bandera. "I love you, Bandera Jefferson."

Their family and friends gathered around them, witnessing the ceremony Hawk led. The answers Bandera and Holly gave seemed to float on the wind.

After he had kissed his bride, he helped her into the hot air balloon, and slowly, they rose into the sky. Holly tossed her bouquet—and Mimi caught it, much to her obvious surprise.

"Now the garter," Bandera said, "the one you tossed through my truck window to start it all."

Holly watched as he took the garter from his pocket, then grinned at her and put it back. "Nah, this one's a keeper," he said. "I bought an extra for those guys down there."

And he tossed it over the side. They laughed when Crockett caught it.

"Never happen," Bandera predicted. "Crockett's got a tougher skull than any of us. No woman will crack him."

Holly pulled him to her so that she could kiss him on the lips. "I love you," she said.

"I love you more than I can ever say," Bandera replied, and the balloon floated away into the pink sunset over Malfunction Junction.

"Well, that's that," Mason said, looking over at Hawk and Jellyfish. "You'd think a marrying fever had hit this ranch."

Hawk gazed at him. "Do you want to know what we learned about your father before or after you eat your piece of wedding cake?"

Don't miss the next Jefferson family adventure.
Turn the page for a sneak preview of
CROCKETT'S SEDUCTION,

available September 2005.
Only from Harlequin American Romance.

Crockett Jefferson was busy looking at the fiery little redhead, Valentine, when he heard the news about his father, Maverick. With regret he took his eyes off of her—she was holding his little niece, Annette, and a box of heart-shaped petits fours she'd made for his brother's wedding.

Being an artist, he appreciated both her lovely baked goods and her beauty. Valentine smiled at him, her pretty blue eyes encouraging, her mouth bowing sweetly, and his heart turned over.

She could never know how he felt about her.

Hawk and Jellyfish—the amateur detectives and family friends who'd found out new information about Maverick—moved under a tree with the oldest Jefferson brother, Mason. Crockett followed.

"We were able to confirm that Maverick was in Alaska for a very long time," Hawk said. "Your father lived with an Alaskan woman of Eskimo descent. She found him slumped in a boat one day, floating offshore. Not knowing who he was or where he'd come from, she had friends help her carry him to her home. When he awakened, Maverick had no memory. Living in a remote area, the woman, Mannie, kept him with her for four years, always hoping he might tell her something about himself."

Hawk looked at Mason, who surely felt the same lead in the pit of his stomach that Crockett did. He was relieved that some trace of Maverick had been found—but he also knew there was more to the story.

Jellyfish put a hand on Mason's shoulder. "You should know that Maverick only told Mannie a few things about himself. She awakened one day to find him gone. He'd left behind enough food to keep her for a long time. Gifts, but not his heart. He was a natural wanderer. During the entire four years he'd stayed with her, she'd sensed he wasn't really with her by the distant look in his eyes as he searched the horizon."

"Oh, jeez," Crockett murmured. They were *all* wanderers.

"Maybe there is more to learn," Hawk said. "But we felt it was important to come home and let you know the good news, and then decide what more you need to learn of your father."

Crockett felt a deep tug in his chest. Now they would hold a family council to decide what to do. It was good they'd found out now, since all the brothers were at the ranch for the annual Fourth of July gathering. Mason wanted the family together at least twice a year—Christmas in the winter and Fourth of July in summer.

In July, the pond was warm enough for the children to swim, Mason had said. But Crockett knew his request really had nothing to do with pond water. Mason just wanted the brothers and their families together, on Malfunction Junction Ranch, their home.

Crockett had to admit there was something to the power of family bonding as he watched Valentine help her tiny daughter across the field. But right now, he wanted to get away from all thoughts of family— and Maverick. It simply hurt too much to know their father had been living on whale meat in a hut somewhere. It was life, but it wasn't life with them.

"Thanks, guys," he murmured to Hawk and Jellyfish, since Mason seemed dumbstruck. "I'm sure Mason will call a family council after dinner. Stick around. There's going to be ribs and sweet peas, grilled corn, and I believe Valentine whipped up some blueberry pies."

That said, he headed in Valentine's direction. He grabbed the box of petits fours from her so that she could play with Annette. "Go on," he told Valentine. "You jump, too."

"Thank you." She pulled off her shoes and climbed inside a structure made for jumping. She bounced gently with her daughter.

With pleasure, he noted that *all* of Valentine bounced. Her hair, her breasts, even her laughter seemed to go up and down as she played with her daughter. He loved watching her be a mother.

Crockett lowered his head for a second, pushing his cowboy hat down as he thought. Before his brother Calhoun had stolen his thunder by becoming a more commercial artist than him, Crockett had painted. It was a good life—cowboying by day, painting by night.

But now all he seemed to think about was Valentine.

She turned and fell over, laughing. Her jeans-clad bottom jiggled and so did her daughter—but it was the fanny that caught his artistic eye.

He'd never seen anything with such rounded perfection. Bountiful and sexy. Lush and full.

"Only sculpting would do that form justice," he said.

"What?" Valentine asked, sitting up to look at him. "Do you want to join us?"

His mind ablaze with creative thoughts, a new idea and a fierce desire to be near her, Crockett set the petits fours on the ground, pulled off his boots and got inside the inflatable house. Annette laughed at him because he was unstable, not used to being on something jiggly, so he put his hands down and pushed on the floor to make her pop up like a gopher.

Valentine and Annette playfully pushed back, catching him off guard. This time, it was Crockett who flew—right into Valentine's lap.

Welcome to the world of American Romance!
Turn the page for exerpts from our July 2005 titles.

A SOLDIER'S RETURN
by Judy Christenberry
TEMPORARY DAD
by Laura Marie Altom
THE BABY SCHEME
by Jacqueline Diamond
A TEXAS STATE OF MIND
by Ann DeFee

We hope you enjoy every one of these books!

Bestselling author and reader favorite Judy Christenberry delivers another emotion-filled family drama from her Children of Texas miniseries, with *A Soldier's Return*. Witness a touching reunion when the Barlow sisters meet their long-lost older brother, and find out how the heart of this brooding warrior is healed by an irrepressible beauty—an extended member of his rediscovered family.

Carrie Abrams was working on her computer when she heard the door of the detective agency open.

She turned her body to greet the entrant, but her head was still glued to the computer screen. When she reluctantly brought her gaze to focus on the tall man with straight posture standing by the door wearing a dress uniform, she gasped.

"Jim! I mean, uh, sorry, I mistook you for someone I—um, may I help you?" She abandoned her clumsy beginning and became as stiff as he was.

"I need to speak with Will Greenfield."

"And your name?" She almost held her breath.

"Captain James Barlow."

"Thank you, Captain Barlow. Just one moment, please."

She got up from her desk, wishing she'd worn a business suit instead of jeans. *You're being silly.* Jim Barlow wouldn't care what she was wearing. He didn't even know her.

She rapped on Will's door, opened it and stepped inside.

"He's here!" She whispered so the man in the outer office wouldn't hear her.

"Who—" Will started to ask, but Carrie didn't wait.

"Jim! He's here. He's wearing his uniform. He wants to speak to you."

Will's face broke into a smile. "Well, show him in!"

Carrie opened the door. "Captain Barlow, please come in."

She wanted to stay in Will's office, but she knew he wouldn't extend the invitation. And she wouldn't ask. It wouldn't be professional.

As she leaned against the door, reluctant to break contact with the two men inside, her gaze roamed her desk.

"Oh, no!" she gasped, and rushed forward. Jim's

picture. Had he seen it? She hoped not. How could she explain her fascination with Vanessa's oldest brother? She'd been enthralled by his square-jawed image, just as Vanessa had been. He was the picture of protective, strong…safe. The big brother every little girl dreamed of.

Her best friend, Vanessa Shaw, had probably dreamed those dreams while being raised as an only child. Then, after her father's death, her mother had told her she had five siblings. That revelation had set in motion a lot of changes in their lives.

Carrie drew a deep breath. It was so tempting to call Vanessa and break the news. But she couldn't do that. That was Will's privilege.

All she could do was sit here and pretend indifference that Jim Barlow had returned to the bosom of his family after twenty-three years.

Temporary Dad is the kind of story American Romance readers love—with moments that will make you laugh (and a moment now and then that'll bring you to tears). Jed Hale is an all-American hero: a fireman, a rescuer, a family man. And Annie Harris is just the woman for him. Join these two on their road trip from Oklahoma to Colorado, with three babies in tow (his triplet niece and nephews, temporarily in his care). Enjoy their various roadside stops—like the Beer Can Cow and the Giant Corncob. And smile as they fall in love….

Waaaaaaaaaaaaaaa! Waa huh waaaaaaaaaAAAHH!

From a cozy rattan chair on the patio of her new condo, Annie Harris looked up from the August issue of *Budget Decorating* and frowned.

Waaaaaaaaaaa!

Granted, she wasn't yet a mother herself, but she had been a preschool teacher for the past seven years, so that did lend her a certain credibility where children were concerned.

WAAAAA HA waaaaaaa!

Annie sighed.

She thought whoever was in charge of that poor, pitiful wailer in the condo across the breezeway from hers ought to try something to calm the infant. Never had she heard so much commotion. Was the poor thing sick?

WAAAAAAAAA WAAAAAAA WAAAAAAA!

WAAAAAAA Huh WAAAAA!

WAAAAAAAAAAAA!

Annie slapped the magazine back to her knees.

Something about the sound of that baby wasn't right.

Was there more than one?

Definitely two.

Maybe even three.

But she'd moved in a couple weeks earlier and hadn't heard a peep or seen signs of any infant in the complex—let alone three—which was partially why she'd chosen this unit over the one beside the river that had had much better views of the town of Pecan, Oklahoma.

WAAAAAA Huh WAAAAAAAAAA!

Again Annie frowned.

No good parent would just leave an infant to cry like this. Could something else be going on? Could the baby's mom or dad be hurt?

Annie popped the latch on her patio gate, creeping across grass not quite green or brown, but a weary shade somewhere in between.

WAAAAAAAAAA!

She crept farther across the shared lawn, stepping onto the weathered brick breezeway she shared with the as-yet-unseen owner of the unit across from hers.

The clubhouse manager—Veronica, a bubbly redhead with a penchant for eighties rock and yogurt— said a bachelor fireman lived there.

Judging by the dead azalea bushes on either side of his front door, Annie hoped the guy was better at watering burning buildings than poor, thirsty plants!

Waaaaaa Huhhhh WAAAA!

She looked at the fireman's door, then her own.

Whatever was going on inside his home probably wasn't any of her business.

WaaaaaAAAAA!

Call her a busybody, but enough was enough.

She just couldn't bear standing around listening to a helpless baby—maybe even more than one helpless baby—cry.

Her first knock on the bachelor fireman's door was gentle. Ladylike. That of a concerned neighbor.

When that didn't work, she gave the door a few good, hard thuds.

She was just about to investigate the French doors on the patio that matched her own when the forest-green front door flew open—"Patti? Where the?— Oh, sorry. Thought you were my sister."

Annie gaped.

What else could she do faced with the handsomest man she'd ever seen hugging not one baby, not two babies, but three?

Like Alli Gardner, the heroine of *The Baby Scheme*, Jacqueline Diamond knows about newspapers. She worked as an Associated Press reporter for many years. You'll love this story of a woman who puts her investigative talents to the test—together with a very attractive private investigator—as the two try to unravel a blackmail scheme targeting parents who've adopted babies from a Central American orphanage.

"I'm here about the story in this morning's paper," Alli said to her managing editor. "The one concerning Mayor LeMott."

"Ned tells me you were working on something similar." J.J. eased into his seat. "He says Payne warned him you might have a complaint."

"It wasn't similar. This *is* my story," Alli told him. "Word for word."

"But you hadn't filed it yet."

"I'd written it but I was holding off so I could double-check a couple of points," she explained. "And there's a sidebar I didn't have time to complete. Mr. Morosco, Payne's planted spyware in my laptop. He stole every bit of that from me."

The editor's forehead wrinkled. He'd been working such long hours he'd begun to lose his tan and had put on a few pounds, she noted. "The two of you have never gotten along, have you? He'd only been here a month when you accused him of stealing your notebook."

"It disappeared from my desk right after he passed by, and the next day he turned in a story based on my research!"

"A guard found your notebook outside that afternoon, right next to where you usually park," the M.E. said.

"I didn't drop it. I'm not that careless." Alli hated being put on the defensive. "Look, you can talk to any of the people I quoted in today's story and they'll confirm who did the reporting."

"Except that most of your sources spoke anonymously," he pointed out.

"I was going to identify them to Ned when I handed it in!" That was standard procedure. "Besides, since when does this paper assign two people to the same story?"

She'd heard of a few big papers that ran their operations in such a cutthroat manner, but the *Outlook* couldn't afford such a waste of staff time. Besides, that kind of competition did horrible things to morale.

"He says Payne asked if he could pursue the same subject. He decided to let the kid show what he could do, and he beat you to the punch."

How could she win when the assistant managing editor was stabbing her in the back? If she were in J.J.'s seat, she probably wouldn't believe her, either.

"Give Payne his own assignment, something he can't steal from anyone else," she said. "He'll blow it."

"As it happens, he's going to have plenty of chances." J.J. fiddled with some papers. "I'm sure you're aware that I've streamlined two other sections. In the meantime, the publisher and Ned and I have been tossing around ideas for the news operation. I'm about to put those proposals into effect."

Why was he telling her this? Allie wondered uneasily. And why was he avoiding her gaze?

"The publisher believes we've got too much duplication and dead wood," he went on. "Some of the older staff members will be asked to take early retirement, but I'm going to have to cut deeper. After careful consideration, I'm afraid we have to let you go."

American Romance is delighted to introduce a brand-new author. You'll love Ann DeFee's sassy humor, her high-energy writing and her *really* entertaining characters. She'll make you laugh—and occasionally gasp. And she'll take you to a Texas town you'll never want to leave. (Fortunately you can visit Port Serenity again next June!)

Oooh, boy! Lolly raised her Pepsi in a tribute to Meg Ryan. Could that girl fake the big O! Lord knows Lolly had perfected the very same skill before Wendell, her ex, hightailed it out to Las Vegas to find fame and fortune as a drummer. Good old Wendell—more frog than prince. But to give credit where credit was due, he *had* managed to sire two of the most fantastic kids in the world.

Nowadays she didn't have to worry about Wendell's flagging ego or, for that matter, any of his other wilting body parts. Celibacy had some rewards—not many, but a few.

Meg had just segued from the throes of parodied passion to a big smile when Lolly's cell phone rang.

"Great, just great," Lolly muttered. She thumped her Pepsi on the coffee table.

"Chief, I hate to call you right at supper time, but I figured you'd want to handle this one. I just got a call from Bud out at the Peaceful Cove Inn, and he's got hisself something of a problem." An after-hours call from the Port Serenity Police Department's gravel-voiced night dispatcher signaled the end to her evening of popcorn and chick flicks.

Chief of police Lavinia "Lolly" Lee Hamilton LaTullipe sighed. Her hectic life as a single mom and head of a small police force left her with very little free time, and when she had a few moments, she wanted to spend them at home with Amanda and Bren, not out corralling scumbags.

"Cletus is on duty tonight, and that man can handle anything short of a full-scale riot," Lolly argued, even though she knew her objections were futile.

Lordy. She'd rather eat Aunt Sissy's fruitcake than abandon the comfort of her living room, especially when Meg was about to find Mr. Right. Lolly hadn't even been able to find Mr. Sorta-Right, though she'd given it the good old college try. Wendell looked pretty good on the outside, but inside he was like an overripe watermelon—mushy and tasteless. Too bad she hadn't noticed that shortcoming when they started dating in high school. Back then his antics were cute; at thirty-seven they weren't quite so appealing.

"I'd really rather not go out tonight."

"Yes, ma'am. I understand. But this one involves Precious." The dispatcher chuckled when Lolly groaned.

Precious was anything but precious. She was the seventeen-year-old demon daughter of Mayor Lance Barton, Lolly's boss and a total klutz in the single-dad department. She and Lance had been buddies since kindergarten, so without a doubt she'd be making an unwanted trip to the Peaceful Cove Inn.

"Oh, man. What did I do to deserve that brat in my life?" Lolly rubbed her forehead in a vain attempt to ward off the headache she knew was coming. "Okay, what's she done now?"

"Seems she's out there with some guys Bud don't know, and she's got a snoot full. He figured we'd want to get her home before someone saw her."

Lolly sighed. "All right, I'll run out and see what I can do. Call her daddy and tell him what's happening."

She muttered an expletive as she marched to the rolltop desk in the kitchen to retrieve her bag, almost tripping over Harvey, the family's gigantic mutt. She strapped on an ankle holster and then checked her

Taser and handcuffs. In this business, a girl had to be prepared.

Amanda, her ten-year-old daughter, was immersed in homework, and as usual, her fourteen-year-old son had his head poked inside the refrigerator.

"Bren, get Amanda to help you with the kitchen." Lolly stopped him as he tried to sneak out of the room and nodded at the open dishwasher and pile of dishes in the sink. "I've got to go out for a few minutes. If you need anything call Mee Maw."

Her firstborn rolled his eyes. "Aw, Mom."

Lolly suppressed the urge to laugh, and instead employed the dreaded raised eyebrow. The kid was in dire need of a positive male role model. Someone stable, upright, respectable and…safe. Yeah, safe. It was time to find a nice, reliable prince—an orthodontist might be good, considering Amanda's overbite.

"I'm leaving. You guys be good," Lolly called out as she opened the screen door.

**The bigger the family, the greater the love—
and the more people trying to ruin your life!**

A TEXAS STATE OF MIND
by Ann DeFee
(HAR #1076)

Single mother of two Lavinia "Lolly" LaTullipe
has plenty to do as police chief of the little
Texas town of Port Serenity. But her job
becomes even more complicated when
Christian Delacroix, an undercover DEA cop,
comes to town to help solve a case. When he
and Lolly meet, the sparks fly—literally!

Available July 2005.

eHARLEQUIN.com

The Ultimate Destination for Women's Fiction

**The ultimate destination for women's fiction.
Visit eHarlequin.com today!**

GREAT BOOKS:
- We've got something for everyone—and at great low prices!
- Choose from new releases, backlist favorites, Themed Collections and preview upcoming books, too.
- Favorite authors: Debbie Macomber, Diana Palmer, Susan Wiggs and more!

EASY SHOPPING:
- Choose our convenient "bill me" option. No credit card required!
- Easy, secure, 24-hour shopping from the comfort of your own home.
- Sign-up for free membership and get $4 off your first purchase.
- Exclusive online offers: FREE books, bargain outlet savings, hot deals.

EXCLUSIVE FEATURES:
- Try Book Matcher—finding your favorite read has never been easier!
- Save & redeem Bonus Bucks.
- Another reason to love Fridays— Free Book Fridays!

Shop online
at www.eHarlequin.com today!

INTBB204R

HARLEQUIN®

AMERICAN *Romance*®

Fatherhood

Fatherhood: what really defines a man.

It's the one thing all women admire in a man—
a willingness to be responsible for a child and
to care for that child with tenderness and love.

Meet two men who are true fathers
in every sense of the word!

Eric Norvald is devoted to his seven-year-old
daughter, Phoebe. But can he give her what she
really wants—a mommy? Find out in

Pamela Browning's
THE MOMMY WISH (AR #1070)

Available June 2005.

In
Laura Marie Altom's
TEMPORARY DAD (AR #1074),

Annie Harnesberry has sworn off men—especially
single fathers. But when her neighbor—a gorgeous
male—needs help with his triplet five-month-old
niece and nephews, Annie can't resist offering
her assistance.

Available July 2005.

COMING NEXT MONTH

#1073 A SOLDIER'S RETURN by Judy Christenberry
Children of Texas
Ever since he was a kid and his orphaned family split, sending him into
foster care, Captain James Barlow knew he was a jinx to anyone he loved.
He'd hidden out safely in the marines…until a detective found him and most of
his siblings. The captain had seen battle, but no enemy made him uneasy like his
newfound family—and the beautiful Carrie Rand.

#1074 TEMPORARY DAD by Laura Marie Altom
Fatherhood
After her last "romantic" experience, Annie Harnesberry has sworn off men—
especially single fathers. Now she just wants to start her new job and redecorate
her condo. But when her neighbor—of the gorgeous male variety—needs help
with his five-month-old triplet niece and nephews, it's Annie who can't seem to
help *herself*.…

#1075 THE BABY SCHEME by Jacqueline Diamond
Alli Gardner may be out of her reporter's job thanks to an underhanded
competitor on her newspaper, but she's not out of story ideas—or an
investigative partner. She and hard-nosed private detective Kevin Vickers
are about to have their hands full looking into a blackmail scheme involving
babies from a Central American orphanage. Soon Alli and Kevin will also
have their hands full with each other.…

#1076 A TEXAS STATE OF MIND by Ann DeFee
Lavinia "Lolly" LaTullipe, a single mother of two, is busy enough as police
chief of the little Texas town of Port Serenity, but her job becomes even
more complicated when the bodies of drug dealers start floating into the
town's cove. Enter Christian Delacroix, undercover DEA cop sent to help
solve the murders. When he and Lolly meet the sparks fly—literally!

www.eHarlequin.com